SUCH A PRETTY
LITTLE PICTURE

and Other Stories

SUCH A PRETTY LITTLE PICTURE
and Other Stories

DOVER THRIFT EDITIONS

Dorothy Parker

DOVER PUBLICATIONS
GARDEN CITY, NEW YORK

DOVER THRIFT EDITIONS

GENERAL EDITOR: SUSAN L. RATTINER
EDITOR OF THIS VOLUME: MICHAEL CROLAND

Bibliographical Note

This Dover edition, first published in 2023, is a new selection of twelve stories reprinted from standard texts. A new introductory Note has been specially prepared for this volume. Readers should be forewarned that the text contains racial and cultural references of the era in which it was written and may be deemed offensive by today's standards.

Library of Congress Cataloging-in-Publication Data

Names: Parker, Dorothy, 1893–1967, author.
Title: Such a pretty little picture and other stories / Dorothy Parker.
Description: Garden City, New York : Dover Publications, 2023. | Series: Dover thrift editions | Summary: "Dorothy Parker's literary prowess reveals a razor-sharp wit in this original collection of twelve short stories, published between 1922 and 1927 in the top literary magazines of the day. These superbly crafted satirical stories, rich with keen insights into human nature, illuminate the pretentious absurdities within relationships between men and women in and outside of marriage, the politics of patriarchy and power, the subordination of women, and observations of class and race"—Provided by publisher.
Identifiers: LCCN 2022040462 | ISBN 9780486851051 (trade paperback)
Subjects: LCGFT: Short stories.
Classification: LCC PS3531.A5855 S78 2023 | DDC 813/.52—dc23/eng/20221007
LC record available at https://lccn.loc.gov/2022040462

Manufactured in the United States of America
85105201   2023
www.doverpublications.com

Note

DOROTHY PARKER, NÉE Rothschild, was born in West End, New Jersey, in 1893. She lived and attended school in New Jersey and New York City. Her formal education ended at fourteen, and she did not receive a high school diploma.

Parker started an editorial job at *Vogue* at twenty-two before becoming a drama critic for *Vanity Fair*. She helped found the Algonquin Round Table, a gathering of writers who ate lunch together and had witty, intellectual discussions. Through that group, she built her reputation as one of New York's most brilliant conversationalists, epitomizing the liberated woman of the 1920s. When *The New Yorker* got its start in 1925, Parker was on the editorial board. For much of her career, she contributed poetry and fiction to the magazine, in addition to book reviews as the "Constant Reader." She published the first of several poetry collections, *Enough Rope*, in 1926.

The present volume collects twelve of Parker's earliest short stories, which appeared in the top literary magazines of the day. The stories were originally published in *American Mercury*, *The New Republic*, *The New Yorker*, *Pictorial Review*, and *Smart Set* between 1922 and 1927. Her fiction conveyed both comedic and tragic perspectives, addressing big issues such as gender roles, poverty, and racial discrimination with razor-sharp wit and keen observation.

Parker won the O. Henry Award for the best short story with the autobiographical "Big Blonde" in 1929. She published collections of her short stories, *Laments for the Living* (1930) and *After Such Pleasures* (1933), which were combined as *Here Lies* (1939).

In 1933, Parker and her second husband, Alan Campbell, moved to Hollywood. They collaborated on writing more than fifteen films, including the Academy Award–nominated *A Star Is Born* (1937).

Parker was inducted into the American Academy of Arts and Letters in 1959. She was a visiting professor at California State College in Los Angeles in 1963. She died of a heart attack in 1967. As a strong supporter of civil rights, she bequeathed most of her estate to Dr. Martin Luther King Jr. When he was assassinated less than a year later, it passed to the National Association for the Advancement of Colored People.

Contents

Contents

SUCH A PRETTY LITTLE PICTURE

and Other Stories

SUCH A PRETTY LITTLE PICTURE

MR. WHEELOCK WAS clipping the hedge. He did not dislike doing it. If it had not been for the faintly sickish odor of the privet bloom, he would definitely have enjoyed it. The new shears were so sharp and bright, there was such a gratifying sense of something done as the young green stems snapped off and the expanse of tidy, square hedge-top lengthened. There was a lot of work to be done on it. It should have been attended to a week ago, but this was the first day that Mr. Wheelock had been able to get back from the city before dinnertime.

Clipping the hedge was one of the few domestic duties that Mr. Wheelock could be trusted with. He was notoriously poor at doing anything around the house. All the suburb knew about it. It was the source of all Mrs. Wheelock's jokes. Her most popular anecdote was of how, the past winter, he had gone out and hired a man to take care of the furnace, after a seven-years' losing struggle with it. She had an admirable memory, and often as she had related the story, she never dropped a word of it. Even now, in the late summer, she could hardly tell it for laughing.

When they were first married, Mr. Wheelock had lent himself to the fun. He had even posed as being more inefficient than he really was, to make the joke better. But he had tired of his helplessness, as a topic of conversation. All the men of Mrs. Wheelock's acquaintance, her cousins, her brother-in-law, the boys she went to high school with, the neighbors' husbands, were adepts at putting up a shelf, at repairing a lock, or making a shirtwaist box. Mr. Wheelock had begun to feel that there was something rather effeminate about his lack of interest in such things.

He had wanted to answer his wife, lately, when she enlivened some neighbor's dinner table with tales of his inadequacy with hammer

1

and wrench. He had wanted to cry, "All right, suppose I'm not any good at things like that. What of it?"

He had played with the idea, had tried to imagine how his voice would sound, uttering the words. But he could think of no further argument for his case than that "What of it?" And he was a little relieved, somehow, at being able to find nothing stronger. It made it reassuringly impossible to go through with the plan of answering his wife's public railleries.

Mrs. Wheelock sat, now, on the spotless porch of the neat stucco house. Beside her was a pile of her husband's shirts and drawers, the price-tags still on them. She was going over all the buttons before he wore the garments, sewing them on more firmly. Mrs. Wheelock never waited for a button to come off, before sewing it on. She worked with quick, decided movements, compressing her lips each time the thread made a slight resistance to her deft jerks.

She was not a tall woman, and since the birth of her child she had gone over from a delicate plumpness to a settled stockiness. Her brown hair, though abundant, grew in an uncertain line about her forehead. It was her habit to put it up in curlers at night, but the crimps never came out in the right place. It was arranged with perfect neatness, yet it suggested that it had been done up and got over with as quickly as possible. Passionately clean, she was always redolent of the germicidal soap she used so vigorously. She was wont to tell people, somewhat redundantly, that she never employed any sort of cosmetics. She had unlimited contempt for women who sought to reduce their weight by dieting, cutting from their menus such nourishing items as cream and puddings and cereals.

Adelaide Wheelock's friends—and she had many of them—said of her that there was no nonsense about her. They and she regarded it as a compliment.

Sister, the Wheelocks' five-year-old daughter, played quietly in the gravel path that divided the tiny lawn. She had been known as Sister since her birth, and her mother still laid plans for a brother for her. Sister's baby carriage stood waiting in the cellar, her baby clothes were stacked expectantly away in bureau drawers. But raises were infrequent at the advertising agency where Mr. Wheelock was employed, and his present salary had barely caught up to the cost of their living. They could not conscientiously regard themselves as being able to afford a son. Both Mr. and Mrs. Wheelock keenly felt his guilt in keeping the bassinet empty.

Sister was not a pretty child, though her features were straight, and her eyes would one day be handsome. The left one turned slightly in toward the nose, now, when she looked in a certain direction; they would operate as soon as she was seven. Her hair was pale and limp, and her color bad. She was a delicate little girl. Not fragile in a picturesque way, but the kind of child that must be always undergoing treatment for its teeth and its throat and obscure things in its nose. She had lately had her adenoids removed, and she was still using squares of surgical gauze instead of handkerchiefs. Both she and her mother somehow felt that these gave her a sort of prestige.

She was additionally handicapped by her frocks, which her mother bought a size or so too large, with a view to Sister's growing into them—an expectation which seemed never to be realized, for her skirts were always too long, and the shoulders of her little dresses came halfway down to her thin elbows. Yet, even discounting the unfortunate way she was dressed, you could tell, in some way, that she was never going to wear any kind of clothes well.

Mr. Wheelock glanced at her now and then as he clipped. He had never felt any fierce thrills of father-love for the child. He had been disappointed in her when she was a pale, large-headed baby, smelling of stale milk and warm rubber. Sister made him feel ill at ease, vaguely irritated him. He had had no share in her training; Mrs. Wheelock was so competent a parent that she took the places of both of them. When Sister came to him to ask his permission to do something, he always told her to wait and ask her mother about it.

He regarded himself as having the usual paternal affection for his daughter. There were times, indeed, when she had tugged sharply at his heart—when he had waited in the corridor outside the operating room; when she was still under the anesthetic, and lay little and white and helpless on her high hospital bed; once when he had accidentally closed a door upon her thumb. But from the first he had nearly acknowledged to himself that he did not like Sister as a person.

Sister was not a whining child, despite her poor health. She had always been sensible and well-mannered, amenable about talking to visitors, rigorously unselfish. She never got into trouble, like other children. She did not care much for other children. She had heard herself described as being "old-fashioned," and she knew she was delicate, and she felt that these attributes rather set her above them. Besides, they were rough and careless of their bodily well-being.

Sister was exquisitely cautious of her safety. Grass, she knew, was often apt to be damp in the late afternoon, so she was careful now to stay right in the middle of the gravel path, sitting on a folded newspaper and playing one of her mysterious games with three petunias that she had been allowed to pick. Mrs. Wheelock never had to speak to her twice about keeping off wet grass, or wearing her rubbers, or putting on her jacket if a breeze sprang up. Sister was an immediately obedient child, always.

II

Mrs. Wheelock looked up from her sewing and spoke to her husband. Her voice was high and clear, resolutely good-humored. From her habit of calling instructions from her upstairs window to Sister playing on the porch below, she spoke always a little louder than was necessary.

"Daddy," she said.

She had called him Daddy since some eight months before Sister was born. She and the child had the same trick of calling his name and then waiting until he signified that he was attending before they went on with what they wanted to say.

Mr. Wheelock stopped clipping, straightened himself and turned toward her.

"Daddy," she went on, thus reassured, "I saw Mr. Ince down at the post office today when Sister and I went down to get the ten o'clock mail—there wasn't much, just a card for me from Grace Williams from that place they go to up on Cape Cod, and an advertisement from some department store or other about their summer fur sale (as if I cared!), and a circular for you from the bank. I opened it; I knew you wouldn't mind.

"Anyway, I just thought I'd tackle Mr. Ince first as last about getting in our cordwood. He didn't see me at first—though I'll bet he really saw me and pretended not to—but I ran right after him. 'Oh, Mr. Ince!' I said. 'Why, hello, Mrs. Wheelock,' he said, and then he asked for you, and I told him you were finely, and everything. Then I said, 'Now, Mr. Ince,' I said, 'how about getting in that cordwood of ours?' And he said, 'Well, Mrs. Wheelock,' he said, 'I'll get it in soon's I can, but I'm short of help right now,' he said.

"Short of help! Of course I couldn't say anything, but I guess he could tell from the way I looked at him how much I believed it. I just said, 'All right, Mr. Ince, but don't you forget us. There may be a cold snap coming on,' I said, 'and we'll be wanting a fire in the living-room. Don't you forget us,' I said, and he said, no, he wouldn't.

"If that wood isn't here by Monday, I think you ought to do something about it, Daddy. There's no sense in all this putting it off, and putting it off. First thing you know there'll be a cold snap coming on, and we'll be wanting a fire in the living-room, and there we'll be! You'll be sure and 'tend to it, won't you, Daddy? I'll remind you again Monday, if I can think of it, but there are so many things!"

Mr. Wheelock nodded and turned back to his clipping—and his thoughts. They were thoughts that had occupied much of his leisure lately. After dinner, when Adelaide was sewing or arguing with the maid, he found himself letting his magazine fall face downward on his knee, while he rolled the same idea round and round in his mind. He had got so that he looked forward, through the day, to losing himself in it. He had rather welcomed the hedge-clipping; you can clip and think at the same time.

It had started with a story that he had picked up somewhere. He couldn't recall whether he had heard it or had read it—that was probably it, he thought, he had run across it in the back pages of some comic paper that someone had left on the train.

It was about a man who lived in a suburb. Every morning he had gone to the city on the 8:12, sitting in the same seat in the same car, and every evening he had gone home to his wife on the 5:17, sitting in the same seat in the same car. He had done this for twenty years of his life. And then one night he didn't come home. He never went back to his office any more. He just never turned up again.

The last man to see him was the conductor on the 5:17.

"He come down the platform at the Grand Central," the man reported, "just like he done every night since I been working on this road. He put one foot on the step, and then he stopped sudden, and he said 'Oh, hell,' and he took his foot off of the step and walked away. And that's the last anybody see of him."

Curious how that story took hold of Mr. Wheelock's fancy. He had started thinking of it as a mildly humorous anecdote; he had come to accept it as fact. He did not think the man's sitting in the same seat in the same car need have been stressed so much. That seemed unimportant. He thought long about the man's wife, wondered what suburb he had lived in. He loved to play with the thing, to try to feel what the man felt before he took his foot off the car's step. He never concerned himself with speculations as to where the man had disappeared, how he had spent the rest of his life. Mr. Wheelock was absorbed in that moment when he had said "Oh, hell," and walked off. "Oh, hell" seemed to Mr. Wheelock a fine thing for him to have said, a perfect summary of the situation.

He tried thinking of himself in the man's place. But no, he would have done it from the other end. That was the real way to do it.

Some summer evening like this, say, when Adelaide was sewing on buttons, up on the porch, and Sister was playing somewhere about. A pleasant, quiet evening it must be, with the shadows lying long on the street that led from their house to the station. He would put down the garden shears, or the hose, or whatever he happened to be puttering with—not throw the thing down, you know, just put it quietly aside—and walk out of the gate and down the street, and that would be the last they'd see of him. He would time it so that he'd just make the 6:03 for the city comfortably.

He did not go ahead with it from there, much. He was not especially anxious to leave the advertising agency forever. He did not particularly dislike his work. He had been an advertising solicitor since he had gone to work at all, and he worked hard at his job and, aside from that, didn't think about it much one way or the other.

It seemed to Mr. Wheelock that before he had got hold of the "Oh, hell" story he had never thought about anything much, one way or the other. But he would have to disappear from the office, too, that was certain. It would spoil everything to turn up there again. He thought dimly of taking a train going West, after the 6:03 got him to the Grand Central Terminal—he might go to Buffalo, say, or perhaps Chicago. Better just let that part take care of itself and go back to dwell on the moment when it would sweep over him that he was going to do it, when he would put down the shears and walk out the gate—

The "Oh, hell" rather troubled him. Mr. Wheelock felt that he would like to retain that; it completed the gesture so beautifully. But he didn't quite know to whom he should say it.

He might stop in at the post office on his way to the station and say it to the postmaster; but the postmaster would probably think he was only annoyed at there being no mail for him. Nor would the conductor of the 6:03, a train Mr. Wheelock never used, take the right interest in it. Of course the real thing to do would be to say it to Adelaide just before he laid down the shears. But somehow Mr. Wheelock could not make that scene come very clear in his imagination.

III

"Daddy," Mrs. Wheelock said briskly.

He stopped clipping, and faced her.

"Daddy," she related, "I saw Doctor Mann's automobile going by the house this morning—he was going to have a look at Mr. Warren, his rheumatism's getting along nicely—and I called him in a minute, to look us over."

She screwed up her face, winked, and nodded vehemently several times in the direction of the absorbed Sister, to indicate that she was the subject of the discourse.

"He said we were going ahead finely," she resumed, when she was sure that he had caught the idea. "Said there was no need for those t-o-n-s-i-l-s to c-o-m-e o-u-t. But I thought, soon's it gets a little cooler, some time next month, we'd just run in to the city and let Doctor Sturges have a look at us. I'd rather be on the safe side."

"But Doctor Lytton said it wasn't necessary, and those doctors at the hospital, and now Doctor Mann, that's known her since she was a baby," suggested Mr. Wheelock.

"I know, I know," replied his wife. "But I'd rather be on the safe side."

Mr. Wheelock went back to his hedge.

Oh, of course he couldn't do it; he never seriously thought he could, for a minute. Of course he couldn't. He wouldn't have the shadow of an excuse for doing it. Adelaide was a sterling woman, an utterly faithful wife, an almost slavish mother. She ran his house economically and efficiently. She harried the suburban trades people into giving them dependable service, drilled the succession of poorly paid, poorly trained maids, cheerfully did the thousand fussy little things that go with the running of a house. She looked after his clothes, gave him medicine when she thought he needed it, oversaw the preparation of every meal that was set before him; they were not especially inspirational meals, but the food was always nourishing and, as a general thing, fairly well cooked. She never lost her temper, she was never depressed, never ill.

Not the shadow of an excuse. People would know that, and so they would invent an excuse for him. They would say there must be another woman.

Mr. Wheelock frowned, and snipped at an obstinate young twig. Good Lord, the last thing he wanted was another woman. What he wanted was that moment when he realized he could do it, when he would lay down the shears—

Oh, of course he couldn't; he knew that as well as anybody. What would they do, Adelaide and Sister? The house wasn't even paid for yet, and there would be that operation on Sister's eye in a couple of years. But the house would be all paid up by next March. And there was always that well-to-do brother-in-law of Adelaide's, the one who, for all his means, put up every shelf in that great big house with his own hands.

Decent people didn't just go away and leave their wives and families that way. All right, suppose you weren't decent; what of it? Here was Adelaide planning what she was going to do when it got a little cooler, next month. She was always planning ahead, always confident that things would go on just the same. Naturally, Mr. Wheelock realized that he couldn't do it, as well as the next one. But there was no harm in fooling around with the idea. Would you say the "Oh, hell" now, before you laid down the shears, or right after? How would it be to turn at the gate and say it?

Mr. and Mrs. Fred Coles came down the street arm-in-arm, from their neat stucco house on the corner.

"See they've got you working hard, eh?" cried Mr. Coles genially, as they paused abreast of the hedge.

Mr. Wheelock laughed politely, marking time for an answer.

"That's right," he evolved.

Mrs. Wheelock looked up from her work, shading her eyes with her thimbled hand against the long rays of the low sun.

"Yes, we finally got Daddy to do a little work," she called brightly. "But Sister and I are staying right here to watch over him, for fear he might cut his little self with the shears."

There was general laughter, in which Sister joined. She had risen punctiliously at the approach of the older people, and she was looking politely at their eyes, as she had been taught.

"And how is my great big girl?" asked Mrs. Coles, gazing fondly at the child.

"Oh, much better," Mrs. Wheelock answered for her. "Doctor Mann says we are going ahead finely. I saw his automobile passing the house this morning—he was going to see Mr. Warren, his rheumatism's coming along nicely—and I called him in a minute to look us over."

She did the wink and the nods, at Sister's back. Mr. and Mrs. Coles nodded shrewdly back at her.

"He said there's no need for those t-o-n-s-i-l-s to c-o-m-e o-u-t," Mrs. Wheelock called. "But I thought, soon's it gets a little cooler, some time next month, we'd just run in to the city and let Doctor Sturges have a look at us. I was telling Daddy, 'I'd rather be on the safe side,' I said."

"Yes, it's better to be on the safe side," agreed Mrs. Coles, and her husband nodded again, sagely this time. She took his arm, and they moved slowly off.

"Been a lovely day, hasn't it?" she said over her shoulder, fearful of having left too abruptly. "Fred and I are taking a little constitutional before supper."

"Oh, taking a little constitutional?" cried Mrs. Wheelock, laughing.

Mrs. Coles laughed also, three or four bars.

"Yes, just taking a little constitutional before supper," she called back.

Sister, weary of her game, mounted the porch, whimpering a little. Mrs. Wheelock put aside her sewing, and took the tired child in her lap. The sun's last rays touched her brown hair, making it a shimmering gold. Her small, sharp face, the thick lines of her figure were in shadow as she bent over the little girl. Sister's head was hidden on her mother's shoulder, the folds of her rumpled white frock followed her limp, relaxed little body.

The lovely light was kind to the cheap, hurriedly built stucco house, to the clean gravel path, and the bits of closely cut lawn. It was gracious, too, to Mr. Wheelock's tall, lean figure as he bent to work on the last few inches of unclipped hedge.

Twenty years, he thought. The man in the story went through with it for twenty years. He must have been a man along around forty-five, most likely. Mr. Wheelock was thirty-seven. Eight years. It's a long time, eight years is. You could easily get so you could say that final "Oh, hell," even to Adelaide, in eight years. It probably wouldn't take more than four for you to know that you could do it. No, not more than two. . . .

Mrs. Coles paused at the corner of the street and looked back at the Wheelocks' house. The last of the light lingered on the mother and child group on the porch, gently touched the tall, white-clad figure of the husband and father as he went up to them, his work done.

Mrs. Coles was a large, soft woman, barren, and addicted to sentiment.

"Look, Fred; just turn around and look at that," she said to her husband. She looked again, sighing luxuriously. "Such a pretty little picture!"

TOO BAD

"MY DEAR," MRS. MARSHALL said to Mrs. Ames, "I never was so surprised in my life. Never in my life. Why, Grace and I were like that—just like *that*."

She held up her right hand, the upstanding first and second fingers rigidly close together, in illustration.

Mrs. Ames shook her head sadly, and offered the cinnamon toast.

"Imagine!" said Mrs. Marshall, refusing it though with a longing eye. "We were going to have dinner with them last Tuesday night, and then I got this letter from Grace from this little place up in Connecticut, saying she was going to be up there she didn't know how long, and she thought, when she came back, she'd probably take just one big room with a kitchenette. Ernest was living down at the club, she said."

"But what did they do about their apartment?" Mrs. Ames's voice was high with anxiety.

"Why, it seems his sister took it, furnished and all—by the way, remind me, I must go and see her," said Mrs. Marshall. "They wanted to move into town, anyway, and they were looking for a place."

"Doesn't she feel terribly about it—his sister?" asked Mrs. Ames.

"Oh—terribly." Mrs. Marshall dismissed the word as inadequate. "My dear, think how everybody that knew them feels. Think how I feel. I don't know when I've had a thing depress me more. If it had been anybody but the Weldons!"

Mrs. Ames nodded.

"That's what I said," she reported.

"That's what everybody says." Mrs. Marshall quickly took away any undeserved credit. "To think of the Weldons separating! Why, I always used to say to Jim. 'Well, there's one happily married couple, anyway,' I used to say, 'so congenial, and with that nice

11

apartment, and all.' And then, right out of a clear sky, they go and separate. I simply can't understand what on earth made them do it. It just seems too awful!"

Again Mrs. Ames nodded, slowly and sadly.

"Yes, it always seems too bad, a thing like that does," she said. "It's too bad."

II

Mrs. Ernest Weldon wandered about the orderly living-room, giving it some of those little feminine touches. She was not especially good as a touch-giver. The idea was pretty, and appealing to her. Before she was married, she had dreamed of herself as moving softly about her new dwelling, deftly moving a vase here or straightening a flower there, and thus transforming it from a house to a home. Even now, after seven years of marriage, she liked to picture herself in the gracious act.

But, though she conscientiously made a try at it every night as soon as the rose-shaded lamps were lit, she was always a bit bewildered as to how one went about performing those tiny miracles that make all the difference in the world to a room. The living-room, it seemed to her, looked good enough as it was—as good as it would ever look, with that mantelpiece and the same old furniture. Delia, one of the most thoroughly feminine of creatures, had subjected it to a long series of emphatic touches earlier in the day, and none of her handiwork had since been disturbed. But the feat of making all the difference in the world, so Mrs. Weldon had always heard, was not a thing to be left to servants. Touch-giving was a wife's job. And Mrs. Weldon was not one to shirk the business she had entered.

With an almost pitiable air of uncertainty, she strayed over to the mantel, lifted a small Japanese vase, and stood with it in her hand, gazing helplessly around the room. The white-enameled bookcase caught her eye, and gratefully she crossed to it and set the vase upon it, carefully rearranging various ornaments to make room. To relieve the congestion, she took up a framed photograph of Mr. Weldon's sister in evening gown and eye-glasses, again looked all about, and then set it timidly on the piano. She smoothed the piano-cover ingratiatingly, straightened the copies of "A Day in Venice," "To a

Wild Rose," and Kreisler's "Caprice Viennois," which stood ever upon the rack, walked over to the tea-table and effected a change of places between the cream-jug and the sugar-bowl.

Then she stepped back, and surveyed her innovations. It was amazing how little difference they made to the room.

Sighing, Mrs. Weldon turned her attention to a bowl of daffodils, slightly past their first freshness. There was nothing to be done there; the omniscient Delia had refreshed them with clear water, had clipped their stems, and removed their more passé sisters. Still Mrs. Weldon bent over them pulling them gently about.

She liked to think of herself as one for whom flowers would thrive, who must always have blossoms about her, if she would be truly happy. When her living-room flowers died, she almost never forgot to stop in at the florist's, the next day, and get a fresh bunch. She told people, in little bursts of confidence, that she loved flowers. There was something almost apologetic in her way of uttering her tender avowal, as if she would beg her listeners not to consider her too bizarre in her taste. It seemed rather as though she expected the hearer to fall back, startled, at her words, crying, "Not really! Well, what *are* we coming to?"

She had other little confessions of affection, too, that she made from time to time; always with a little hesitation, as if understandably delicate about baring her heart, she told her love for color, the country, a good time, a really interesting play, nice materials, well-made clothes, and sunshine. But it was her fondness for flowers that she acknowledged oftenest. She seemed to feel that this, even more than her other predilections, set her apart from the general.

Mrs. Weldon gave the elderly daffodils a final pat, now, and once more surveyed the room, to see if any other repairs suggested themselves. Her lips tightened as the little Japanese vase met her gaze; distinctly, it had been better off in the first place. She set it back, the irritation that the sight of the mantel always gave her welling within her.

She had hated the mantelpiece from the moment they had first come to look at the apartment. There were other things that she had always hated about the place, too—the long, narrow hall, the dark dining-room, the inadequate closets. But Ernest had seemed to like the apartment well enough, so she had said nothing, then or since. After all, what was the use of fussing? Probably there would always be drawbacks, wherever they lived. There were enough in the last place they had had.

So they had taken the apartment on a five-year lease—there were four years and three months to go. Mrs. Weldon felt suddenly weary. She lay down on the davenport, and pressed her thin hand against her dull brown hair.

Mr. Weldon came down the street, bent almost double in his battle with the wind from the river. His mind went over its nightly dark thoughts on living near Riverside Drive, five blocks from a subway station—two of those blocks loud with savage gales. He did not much like their apartment, even when he reached it. As soon as he had seen that dining-room, he had realized that they must always breakfast by artificial light—a thing he hated. But Grace had never appeared to notice it, so he had held his peace. It didn't matter much, anyway, he explained to himself. There was pretty sure to be something wrong, everywhere. The dining-room wasn't much worse than that bedroom on the court, in the last place. Grace had never seemed to mind that, either.

Mrs. Weldon opened the door at his ring.

"Well!" she said, cheerily.

They smiled brightly at each other.

"Hel-lo," he said. "Well! You home?"

They kissed, slightly. She watched with polite interest while he hung up his hat and coat, removed the evening papers from his pocket, and handed one to her.

"Bring the papers?" she said, taking it.

She preceded him along the narrow hall to the living-room, where he let himself slowly down into his big chair, with a sound between a sigh and a groan. She sat opposite him, on the davenport. Again they smiled brightly at each other.

"Well, what have you been doing with yourself today?" he inquired.

She had been expecting the question. She had planned before he came in, how she would tell him all the little events of her day—how the woman in the grocer's shop had had an argument with the cashier, and how Delia had tried out a new salad for lunch with but moderate success, and how Alice Marshall had come to tea and it was quite true that Norma Matthews was going to have another baby. She had woven them into a lively little narrative, carefully choosing amusing phrases of description; had felt that she was going to tell it well and with spirit, and that he might laugh at the account of the occurrence in the grocer's. But now, as she considered it, it seemed to her a long, dull story. She had not the energy to begin it. And he was already smoothing out his paper.

"Oh, nothing," she said, with a gay little laugh. "Did you have a nice day?"

"Why—" he began. He had had some idea of telling her how he had finally put through that Detroit thing, and how tickled J. G. had seemed to be about it. But his interest waned, even as he started to speak. Besides, she was engrossed in breaking off a loose thread from the wool fringe on one of the pillows beside her.

"Oh, pretty fair," he said.

"Tired?" she asked.

"Not so much," he answered. "Why—want to do anything tonight?"

"Why, not unless you do," she said, brightly. "Whatever you say."

"Whatever *you* say," he corrected her.

The subject closed. There was a third exchange of smiles, and then he hid most of himself behind his paper.

Mrs. Weldon, too, turned to the newspaper. But it was an off night for news—a long speech of somebody's, a plan for a garbage dump, a proposed dirigible, a four-day-old murder mystery. No one she knew had died or become engaged or married, or had attended any social functions. The fashions depicted on the woman's page were for Miss Fourteen-to-Sixteen. The advertisements ran mostly to bread, and sauces, and men's clothes and sales of kitchen utensils. She put the paper down.

She wondered how Ernest could get so much enjoyment out of a newspaper. He could occupy himself with one for almost an hour, and then pick up another and go all through the same news with unabated interest. She wished that she could. She wished, even more than that, that she could think of something to say. She glanced around the room for inspiration.

"See my pretty daffy-down-dillies?" she said, finding it. To anyone else, she would have referred to them as daffodils.

Mr. Weldon looked in the direction of the flowers.

"M-m-mm," he said in admission, and returned to the news.

She looked at him, and shook her head despondently. He did not see, behind the paper; nor did she see that he was not reading. He was waiting, his hands gripping the printed sheet till their knuckles were blue-white, for her next remark.

It came.

"I love flowers," she said, in one of her little rushes of confidence.

Her husband did not answer. He sighed, his grip relaxed, and he went on reading.

Mrs. Weldon searched the room for another suggestion.

"Ernie," she said, "I'm so comfortable. Wouldn't you like to get up and get my handkerchief off the piano for me?"

He rose instantly. "Why, certainly," he said.

The way to ask people to fetch handkerchiefs, he thought as he went back to his chair, was to ask them to do it, and not try to make them think that you were giving them a treat. Either come right out and ask them, would they or wouldn't they, or else get up and get your handkerchief yourself.

"Thank you ever so much," his wife said with enthusiasm.

Delia appeared in the doorway. "Dinner," she murmured bashfully, as if it were not quite a nice word for a young woman to use, and vanished.

"Dinner, Ern," cried Mrs. Weldon gaily, getting up.

"Just minute," issued indistinctly from behind the newspaper.

Mrs. Weldon waited. Then her lips compressed, and she went over and playfully took the paper from her husband's hands. She smiled carefully at him, and he smiled back at her.

"You go ahead in," he said, rising. "I'll be right with you. I've just got to wash up."

She looked after him, and something like a volcanic eruption took place within her. You'd think that just one night—just one little night—he might go and wash before dinner was announced. Just one night—it didn't seem much to ask. But she said nothing. God knew it was aggravating, but after all, it wasn't worth the trouble of fussing about.

She was waiting, cheerful and bright, courteously refraining from beginning her soup, when he took his place at the table.

"Oh, tomato soup, eh?" he said.

"Yes," she answered. "You like it, don't you?"

"Who—me?" he said. "Oh, yes. Yes, indeed."

She smiled at him.

"Yes, I thought you liked it," she said.

"You like it, too, don't you?" he inquired.

"Oh, yes," she assured him. "Yes, I like it ever so much. I'm awfully fond of tomato soup."

"Yes," he said, "there's nothing much better than tomato soup on a cold night."

She nodded.

"I think it's nice, too," she confided.

They had had tomato soup for dinner probably three times a month during their married life.

The soup was finished, and Delia brought in the meat.

"Well, that looks pretty good," said Mr. Weldon, carving it. "We haven't had steak for a long time."

"Why, yes, we have, too, Ern," his wife said eagerly. "We had it—let me see, what night were the Baileys here?—we had it Wednesday night—no, Thursday night. Don't you remember?"

"Did we?" he said. "Yes, I guess you're right. It seemed longer, somehow."

Mrs. Weldon smiled politely. She could not think of any way to prolong the discussion.

What did married people talk about, anyway, when they were alone together? She had seen married couples—not dubious ones but people she really knew were husbands and wives—at the theater or in trains, talking together as animatedly as if they were just acquaintances. She always watched them, marvelingly, wondering what on earth they found to say.

She could talk well enough to other people. There never seemed to be enough time for her to finish saying all she wanted to to her friends; she recalled how she had run on to Alice Marshall, only that afternoon. Both men and women found her attractive to listen to; not brilliant, not particularly funny, but still amusing and agreeable. She was never at a loss for something to say, never conscious of groping around for a topic. She had a good memory for bits of fresh gossip, or little stories of some celebrity that she had read or heard somewhere, and a knack of telling them entertainingly. Things people said to her stimulated her to quick replies, and more amusing narratives. They weren't especially scintillating people, either; it was just that they talked to her.

That was the trick of it. If nobody said anything to you, how were you to carry on a conversation from there? Inside, she was always bitter and angry at Ernest for not helping her out.

Ernest, too, seemed to be talkative enough when he was with others. People were always coming up and telling her how much they had enjoyed meeting her husband, and what fun he was. They weren't just being polite. There was no reason why they should go out of their way to say it.

Even when she and Ernest had another couple in to dinner or bridge, they both talked and laughed easily, all evening long. But as soon as the guests said good-night and what an awfully nice evening it had been, and the door had closed behind them, there the Weldons were again, without a word to say to each other. It would have been intimate and amusing to have talked over their guests' clothes and skill at bridge and probable domestic and financial affairs, and she would do it the next day, with great interest, too, to Alice Marshall, or some other one of her friends. But she couldn't do it with Ernest. Just as she started to, she found she simply couldn't make the effort.

So they would put away the card-table and empty the ash-receivers, with many "Oh, I beg your pardon's" and "No, no—I was in your way's," and then Ernest would say, "Well, I guess I'll go along to bed," and she would answer, "All right—I'll be in in a minute," and they would smile cheerfully at each other, and another evening would be over.

She tried to remember what they used to talk about before they were married, when they were engaged. It seemed to her that they never had had much to say to each other. But she hadn't worried about it then; indeed, she had felt the satisfaction of the correct, in their courtship, for she had always heard that true love was inarticulate. Then, besides, there had been always kissing and things, to take up your mind. But it had turned out that true marriage was apparently equally dumb. And you can't depend on kisses and all the rest of it to while away the evenings, after seven years.

You'd think that you would get used to it, in seven years, would realize that that was the way it was, and let it go at that. You don't, though. A thing like that gets on your nerves. It isn't one of those cozy, companionable silences that people occasionally fall into together. It makes you feel as if you must do something about it, as if you weren't performing your duty. You have the feeling a hostess has when her party is going badly, when her guests sit in corners and refuse to mingle. It makes you nervous and self-conscious, and you talk desperately about tomato soup, and say things like "daffy-down-dilly."

Mrs. Weldon cast about in her mind for a subject to offer her husband. There was Alice Marshall's new system of reducing—no, that was pretty dull. There was the case she had read in the morning's paper about the man of eighty-seven who had taken, as his fourth wife, a girl of twenty—he had probably seen that, and as long as he hadn't thought it worth repeating, he wouldn't think it worth hearing. There was the thing the Baileys' little boy had said about Jesus—no, she had told him that the night before.

She looked over at him, desultorily eating his rhubarb pie. She wished he wouldn't put that greasy stuff on his head. Perhaps it was necessary, if his hair really was falling out, but it did seem that he might find some more attractive remedy, if he only had the consideration to look around for one. Anyway, why must his hair fall out? There was something a little disgusting about people with falling hair.

"Like your pie, Ernie?" she asked vivaciously.

"Why, I don't know," he said, thinking it over. "I'm not so crazy about rhubarb, I don't think. Are you?"

"No, I'm not so awfully crazy about it," she answered. "But then, I'm not really crazy about any kind of pie."

"Aren't you really?" he said, politely surprised. "I like pie pretty well—some kinds of pie."

"Do you?" The polite surprise was hers now.

"Why, yes," he said. "I like a nice huckleberry pie, or a nice lemon meringue pie, or a—" He lost interest in the thing himself, and his voice died away.

He avoided looking at her left hand, which lay on the edge of the table, palm upward. The long, grey-white ends of her nails protruded beyond the tips of her fingers, and the sight made him uncomfortable. Why in God's name must she wear her finger nails that preposterous length, and file them to those horrible points? If there was anything that he hated, it was a woman with pointed finger nails.

They returned to the living-room, and Mr. Weldon again eased himself down into his chair, reaching for the second paper.

"Quite sure there isn't anything you'd like to do tonight?" he asked solicitously. "Like to go to the movies or anything?"

"Oh, no," she said. "Unless there's something you want to do."

"No, no," he answered. "I just thought maybe you wanted to."

"Not unless you do," she said.

He began on his paper, and she wandered aimlessly about the room. She had forgotten to get a new book from the library, and it had never in her life occurred to her to reread a book that she had once completed. She thought vaguely of playing solitaire, but she did not care enough about it to go to the trouble of getting out the cards, and setting up the table. There was some sewing that she could do, and she thought that she might presently go into the bedroom and fetch the nightgown that she was making for herself. Yes, she would probably do that, in a little while.

Ernest would read industriously, and, along toward the middle of the paper, he would start yawning aloud. Something happened inside Mrs. Weldon when he did this. She would murmur that she had to speak to Delia, and hurry to the kitchen. She would stay there rather a long time, looking vaguely into jars and inquiring half-heartedly about laundry lists, and, when she returned, he would have gone in to get ready for bed.

In a year, three hundred of their evenings were like this. Seven times three hundred is more than two thousand.

Mrs. Weldon went into the bedroom, and brought back her sewing. She sat down, pinned the pink satin to her knee, and began whipping narrow lace along the top of the half-made garment. It was fussy work. The fine thread knotted and drew, and she could not get the light adjusted so that the shadow of her head did not fall on her work. She grew a little sick, from the strain on her eyes.

Mr. Weldon turned a page, and yawned aloud. "Wah-huh-huh-huh-huh," he went, on a descending scale. He yawned again, and this time climbed the scale.

III

"My dear," Mrs. Ames said to Mrs. Marshall, "don't you really think that there must have been some other woman?"

"Oh, I simply couldn't think it was anything like that," said Mrs. Marshall. "Not Ernest Weldon. So devoted—home every night at half-past six, and such good company, and so jolly, and all. I don't see how there *could* have been."

"Sometimes," observed Mrs. Ames, "those awfully jolly men at home are just the kind."

"Yes, I know," Mrs. Marshall said. "But not Ernest Weldon. Why, I used to say to Jim, 'I never saw such a devoted husband in my life,' I said. Oh, not Ernest Weldon."

"I don't suppose," began Mrs. Ames, and hesitated. "I don't suppose," she went on, intently pressing the bit of sodden lemon in her cup with her teaspoon, "that Grace—that there was ever anyone—or anything like that?"

"Oh, Heavens, no," cried Mrs. Marshall. "Grace Weldon just gave her whole life to that man. It was Ernest this and Ernest that every minute. I simply can't understand it. If there was one earthly reason—

if they ever fought, or if Ernest drank, or anything like that. But they got along so beautifully together—why, it just seems as if they must have been crazy to go and do a thing like this. Well, I can't begin to tell you how blue it's made me. It seems so awful!"

"Yes," said Mrs. Ames, "it certainly is too bad."

MR. DURANT

NOT FOR SOME ten days had Mr. Durant known any such ease of mind. He gave himself up to it, wrapped himself, warm and soft, as in a new and an expensive cloak. God, for Whom Mr. Durant entertained a good-humored affection, was in His heaven, and all was again well with Mr. Durant's world.

Curious how this renewed peace sharpened his enjoyment of the accustomed things about him. He looked back at the rubber works, which he had just left for the day, and nodded approvingly at the solid red pile, at the six neat stories rising impressively into the darkness. You would go far, he thought, before you would find a more up-and-coming outfit, and there welled in him a pleasing, proprietary sense of being a part of it.

He gazed amiably down Center Street, noting how restfully the lights glowed. Even the wet, dented pavement, spotted with thick puddles, fed his pleasure by reflecting the discreet radiance above it. And to complete his comfort, the car for which he was waiting, admirably on time, swung into view far down the track. He thought, with a sort of jovial tenderness, of what it would bear him to; of his dinner—it was fish-chowder night—of his children, of his wife, in the order named. Then he turned his kindly attention to the girl who stood near him, obviously awaiting the Center Street car, too. He was delighted to feel a sharp interest in her. He regarded it as being distinctly creditable to himself that he could take a healthy notice of such matters once more. Twenty years younger—that's what he felt.

Rather shabby, she was, in her rough coat with its shagginess rubbed off here and there. But there was a something in the way her cheaply smart turban was jammed over her eyes, in the way her thin young figure moved under the loose coat. Mr. Durant pointed his tongue, and moved it delicately along his cool, smooth upper lip.

The car approached, clanged to a stop before them. Mr. Durant stepped gallantly aside to let the girl get in first. He did not help her to enter, but the solicitous way in which he superintended the process gave all the effect of his having actually assisted her.

Her tight little skirt slipped up over her thin, pretty legs as she took the high step. There was a run in one of her flimsy silk stockings. She was doubtless unconscious of it; it was well back toward the seam, extending, probably from her garter, half-way down the calf. Mr. Durant had an odd desire to catch his thumbnail in the present end of the run, and to draw it on down until the slim line of the dropped stitches reached to the top of her low shoe. An indulgent smile at his whimsy played about his mouth, broadening to a grin of affable evening greeting for the conductor, as he entered the car and paid his fare.

The girl sat down somewhere far up at the front. Mr. Durant found a desirable seat toward the rear, and craned his neck to see her. He could catch a glimpse of a fold of her turban and a bit of her brightly rouged cheek, but only at a cost of holding his head in a strained, and presently painful, position. So, warmed by the assurance that there would always be others, he let her go, and settled himself restfully. He had a ride of twenty minutes or so before him. He allowed his head to fall gently back, to let his eyelids droop, and gave himself to his thoughts. Now that the thing was comfortably over and done with, he could think of it easily, almost laughingly. Last week, now, and even part of the week before, he had had to try with all his strength to force it back every time it wrenched itself into his mind. It had positively affected his sleep. Even though he was shielded by his newly acquired amused attitude, Mr. Durant felt indignation flood within him when he recalled those restless nights.

He had met Rose for the first time about three months before. She had been sent up to his office to take some letters for him. Mr. Durant was assistant manager of the rubber company's credit department; his wife was wont to refer to him as one of the officers of the company, and, though she often spoke thus of him to people in his presence, he never troubled to go more fully into detail about his position. He rated a room, a desk, and a telephone to himself; but not a stenographer. When he wanted to give dictation or to have some letters typewritten, he telephoned around to the various other offices until he found a girl who was not busy with her own work. That was how Rose had come to him.

She was not a pretty girl. Distinctly, no. But there was a rather sweet fragility about her, and an almost desperate timidity that Mr. Durant had once found engaging, but that he now thought of with a prickling irritation. She was twenty, and the glamour of youth was around her. When she bent over her work, her back showing white through her sleazy blouse, her clean hair coiled smoothly on her thin neck, her straight, childish legs crossed at the knee to support her pad, she had an undeniable appeal.

But not pretty—no. Her hair wasn't the kind that went up well, her eyelashes and lips were too pale, she hadn't much knack about choosing and wearing her cheap clothes. Mr. Durant, in reviewing the thing, felt a surprise that she should ever have attracted him. But it was a tolerant surprise, not an impatient one. Already he looked back on himself as being just a big boy in the whole affair.

It did not occur to him to feel even a flicker of astonishment that Rose should have responded so eagerly to him, an immovably married man of forty-nine. He never thought of himself in that way. He used to tell Rose, laughingly, that he was old enough to be her father, but neither of them ever really believed it. He regarded her affection for him as the most natural thing in the world—there she was, coming from a much smaller town, never the sort of girl to have had admirers; naturally, she was dazzled at the attentions of a man who, as Mr. Durant put it, was approaching the prime. He had been charmed with the idea of there having been no other men in her life; but lately, far from feeling flattered at being the first and only one, he had come to regard it as her having taken a sly advantage of him, to put him in that position.

It had all been surprisingly easy. Mr. Durant knew it would be almost from the first time he saw her. That did not lessen its interest in his eyes. Obstacles discouraged him, rather than led him on. Elimination of bother was the main thing.

Rose was not a coquettish girl. She had that curious directness that some very timid people possess. There were her scruples, of course, but Mr. Durant readily reasoned them away. Not that he was a master of technique, either. He had had some experiences, probably a third as many as he habitually thought of himself as having been through, but none that taught him much of the delicate shadings of wooing. But then, Rose's simplicity asked exceedingly little.

She was never one to demand much of him, anyway. She never thought of stirring up any trouble between him and his wife, never besought him to leave his family and go away with her, even for a day. Mr. Durant valued her for that. It did away with a lot of probable fussing.

It was amazing how free they were, how little lying there was to do. They stayed in the office after hours—Mr. Durant found many letters that must be dictated. No one thought anything of that. Rose was busy most of the day, and it was only considerate that Mr. Durant should not break in on her employer's time, only natural that he should want as good a stenographer as she was to attend to his correspondence.

Rose's only relative, a married sister, lived in another town. The girl roomed with an acquaintance named Ruby, also employed at the rubber works, and Ruby, who was much taken up with her own affairs of the emotions, never appeared to think it strange if Rose was late to dinner, or missed the meal entirely. Mr. Durant readily explained to his wife that he was detained by a rush of business. It only increased his importance, to her, and spurred her on to devising especially pleasing dishes, and solicitously keeping them hot for his return. Sometimes, important in their guilt, Rose and he put out the light in the little office and locked the door, to trick the other employees into thinking that they had long ago gone home. But no one ever so much as rattled the doorknob, seeking admission.

It was all so simple that Mr. Durant never thought of it as anything outside the usual order of things. His interest in Rose did not blunt his appreciation of chance attractive legs or provocative glances. It was an entanglement of the most restful, comfortable nature. It even held a sort of homelike quality, for him.

And then everything had to go and get spoiled. "Wouldn't you know?" Mr. Durant asked himself, with deep bitterness.

Ten days before, Rose had come weeping to his office. She had the sense to wait till after hours, for a wonder, but anybody might have walked in and seen her blubbering there; Mr. Durant felt it to be due only to the efficient management of his personal God that no one had. She wept, as he sweepingly put it, all over the place. The color left her cheeks and collected damply in her nose, and rims of vivid pink grew around her pale eyelashes. Even her hair became affected; it came away from the pins, and stray ends of it wandered limply over her neck. Mr. Durant hated to look at her, could not bring himself to touch her.

All his energies were expended in urging her for God's sake to keep quiet; he did not ask her what was the matter. But it came out, between bursts of unpleasant-sounding sobs. She was "in trouble."

Neither then nor in the succeeding days did she and Mr. Durant ever use any less delicate phrase to describe her condition. Even in their thoughts, they referred to it that way.

She had suspected it, she said, for some time, but she hadn't wanted to bother him about it until she was absolutely sure. "Didn't want to bother me!" thought Mr. Durant.

Naturally, he was furious. Innocence is a desirable thing, a dainty thing, an appealing thing, in its place; but carried too far, it is merely ridiculous. Mr. Durant wished to God that he had never seen Rose. He explained this desire to her.

But that was no way to get things done. As he had often jovially remarked to his friends, he knew "a thing or two." Cases like this could be what people of the world called "fixed up"—New York society women, he understood, thought virtually nothing of it. This case could be fixed up, too. He got Rose to go home, telling her not to worry, he would see that everything was all right. The main thing was to get her out of sight, with that nose and those eyes.

But knowing a thing or two and putting the knowledge into practice turned out to be vastly different things. Mr. Durant did not know whom to seek for information. He pictured himself inquiring of his intimates if they could tell him of "someone that this girl he had heard about could go to." He could hear his voice uttering the words, could hear the nervous laugh that would accompany them, the terrible flatness of them as they left his lips. To confide in one person would be confiding in at least one too many. It was a progressing town, but still small enough for gossip to travel like a typhoon. Not that he thought for a moment that his wife would believe any such thing, if it reached her; but where would be the sense in troubling her?

Mr. Durant grew pale and jumpy over the thing as the days went by. His wife worried herself into one of her sick spells over his petulant refusals of second helpings. There daily arose in him an increasing anger that he should be drawn into conniving to find a way to break the law of his country—probably the law of every country in the world. Certainly of every decent, Christian place.

It was Ruby, finally, who got them out of it. When Rose confessed to him that she had broken down and told Ruby, his rage leaped higher than any words. Ruby was secretary to the vice-president of the rubber company. It would be pretty, wouldn't it, if she let it out? He had lain wide-eyed beside his wife all that night through. He shuddered at the thought of chance meetings with Ruby in the hall.

But Ruby had made it delightfully simple, when they did meet. There were no reproachful looks, no cold turnings away of the head. She had given him her usual smiling "good-morning," and added a little upward glance, mischievous, understanding, with just the least hint of admiration in it. There was a sense of intimacy, of a shared secret binding them cozily together. A fine girl, that Ruby!

Ruby had managed it all without any fuss. Mr. Durant was not directly concerned in the planning. He heard of it only through Rose, on the infrequent occasions when he had had to see her. Ruby knew, through some indistinct friends of hers, of "a woman." It would be twenty-five dollars. Mr. Durant had gallantly insisted upon giving Rose the money. She had started to sniffle about taking it, but he had finally prevailed. Not that he couldn't have used the twenty-five very nicely himself, just then, with Junior's teeth, and all!

Well, it was all over now. The invaluable Ruby had gone with Rose to "the woman"; had that very afternoon taken her to the station and put her on a train for her sister's. She had even thought of wiring the sister beforehand that Rose had had influenza and must have a rest.

Mr. Durant had urged Rose to look on it as just a little vacation. He promised, moreover, to put in a good word for her whenever she wanted her job back. But Rose had gone pink about the nose again at the thought. She had sobbed her rasping sobs, then had raised her face from her stringy handkerchief and said, with an entirely foreign firmness, that she never wanted to see the rubber works or Ruby or Mr. Durant again. He had laughed indulgently, had made himself pat her thin back. In his relief at the outcome of things, he could be generous to the pettish.

He chuckled inaudibly, as he reviewed that last scene. "I suppose she thought she'd make me sore, saying she was never coming back," he told himself. "I suppose I was supposed to get down on my knees and coax her."

It was fine to dwell on the surety that it was all done with. Mr. Durant had somewhere picked up a phrase that seemed ideally suited to the occasion. It was to him an admirably dashing expression. There was something stylish about it; it was the sort of thing you would expect to hear used by men who wore spats and swung canes without self-consciousness. He employed it now, with satisfaction.

"Well, that's that," he said to himself. He was not sure that he didn't say it aloud.

Dorothy Parker

The car slowed, and the girl in the rough coat came down toward the door. She was jolted against Mr. Durant—he would have sworn she did it purposely—uttered a word of laughing apology, gave him what he interpreted as an inviting glance. He half rose to follow her, then sank back again. After all, it was a wet night, and his corner was five blocks farther on. Again there came over him the cozy assurance that there would always be others.

In high humor, he left the car at his street, and walked in the direction of his house. It was a mean night, but the insinuating cold and the black rain only made more graphic his picture of the warm, bright house, the great dish of steaming fish chowder, the well-behaved children and wife that awaited him. He walked rather slowly to make them seem all the better for the wait, humming a little on his way down the neat sidewalk, past the solid, reputably shabby houses.

Two girls ran past him, holding their hands over their heads to protect their hats from the wet. He enjoyed the click of their heels on the pavement, their little bursts of breathless laughter, their arms upraised in a position that brought out all the neat lines of their bodies. He knew who they were—they lived three doors down from him, in the house with the lamp-post in front of it. He had often lingeringly noticed their fresh prettiness. He hurried, so that he might see them run up the steps, their narrow skirts sliding up over their legs. His mind went back to the girl with the run in her stocking, and amusing thoughts filled him as he entered his own house.

His children rushed, clamoring, to meet him, as he unlocked the door. There was something exciting going on, for Junior and Charlotte were usually too careful-mannered to cause people discomfort by rushing and babbling. They were nice, sensible children, good at their lessons, and punctilious about brushing their teeth, speaking the truth, and avoiding playmates who used bad words. Junior would be the very picture of his father, when they got the bands off his teeth, and little Charlotte strongly resembled her mother. Friends often commented on what a nice arrangement it was.

Mr. Durant smiled good-naturedly through their racket, carefully hanging up his coat and hat. There was even pleasure for him in the arrangement of his apparel on the cool, shiny knob of the hatrack. Everything was pleasant, tonight. Even the children's noise couldn't irritate him.

Eventually he discovered the cause of the commotion. It was a little stray dog that had come to the back door. They were out in the kitchen helping Freda, and Charlotte thought she heard something scratching, and Freda said nonsense, but Charlotte went to the door, anyway, and there was this little dog, trying to get in out of the wet. Mother helped them give it a bath, and Freda fed it, and now it was in the living-room. Oh, Father, couldn't they keep it, please, couldn't they, couldn't they, please, Father, couldn't they? It didn't have any collar on it—so you see it didn't belong to anybody. Mother said all right, if he said so, and Freda liked it fine.

Mr. Durant still smiled his gentle smile. "We'll see," he said.

The children looked disappointed, but not despondent. They would have liked more enthusiasm, but "we'll see," they knew by experience, meant a leaning in the right direction.

Mr. Durant proceeded to the living-room, to inspect the visitor. It was not a beauty. All too obviously, it was the living souvenir of a mother who had never been able to say no. It was a rather stocky little beast with shaggy white hair and occasional, rakishly placed patches of black. There was a suggestion of Sealyham terrier about it, but that was almost blotted out by hosts of reminiscences of other breeds. It looked, on the whole, like a composite photograph of Popular Dogs. But you could tell at a glance that it had a way with it. Scepters have been tossed aside for that.

It lay, now, by the fire, waving its tragically long tail wistfully, its eyes pleading with Mr. Durant to give it a fair trial. The children had told it to lie down there, and so it did not move. That was something it could do toward repaying them.

Mr. Durant warmed to it. He did not dislike dogs, and he somewhat fancied the picture of himself as a soft-hearted fellow who extended shelter to friendless animals. He bent, and held out a hand to it.

"Well, sir," he said, genially. "Come here, good fellow."

The dog ran to him, wriggling ecstatically. It covered his cold hand with joyous, though respectful kisses, then laid its warm, heavy head on his palm. "You are beyond a doubt the greatest man in America," it told him with its eyes.

Mr. Durant enjoyed appreciation and gratitude. He patted the dog graciously.

"Well, sir, how'd you like to board with us?" he said. "I guess you can plan to settle down." Charlotte squeezed Junior's arm wildly. Neither of them, though, thought it best to crowd their good fortune by making any immediate comment on it.

Mrs. Durant entered from the kitchen, flushed with her final attentions to the chowder. There was a worried line between her eyes. Part of the worry was due to the dinner, and part to the disturbing entrance of the little dog into the family life. Anything not previously included in her day's schedule threw Mrs. Durant into a state resembling that of one convalescing from shellshock. Her hands jerked nervously, beginning gestures that they never finished.

Relief smoothed her face when she saw her husband patting the dog. The children, always at ease with her, broke their silence and jumped about her, shrieking that Father said it might stay.

"There, now—didn't I tell you what a dear, good father you had?" she said in the tone parents employ when they have happened to guess right. "That's fine, Father. With that big yard and all, I think we'll make out all right. She really seems to be an awfully good little——"

Mr. Durant's hand stopped sharply in its patting motions, as if the dog's neck had become red-hot to his touch. He rose, and looked at his wife as at a stranger who had suddenly begun to behave wildly.

"She?" he said. He maintained the look and repeated the word. "She?"

Mrs. Durant's hands jerked.

"Well——" she began, as if about to plunge into a recital of extenuating circumstances. "Well—yes," she concluded.

The children and the dog looked nervously at Mr. Durant, feeling something was gone wrong. Charlotte whimpered wordlessly.

"Quiet!" said her father, turning suddenly upon her. "I said it could stay, didn't I? Did you ever know Father to break a promise?"

Charlotte politely murmured, "No, Father," but conviction was not hers. She was a philosophical child, though, and she decided to leave the whole issue to God, occasionally jogging Him up a bit with prayer.

Mr. Durant frowned at his wife, and jerked his head backward. This indicated that he wished to have a few words with her, for adults only, in the privacy of the little room across the hall, known as "Father's den."

He had directed the decoration of his den, had seen that it had been made a truly masculine room. Red paper covered its walls, up to the wooden rack on which were displayed ornamental steins, of domestic manufacture. Empty pipe-racks—Mr. Durant smoked cigars—were nailed against the red paper at frequent intervals. On one wall was an indifferent reproduction of a drawing of a young woman with wings like a vampire bat, and on another, a watercolored photograph of "September Morn," the tints running a bit beyond the edges of the figure as if the artist's emotions had rendered his hand unsteady. Over the table was carefully flung a tanned and fringed hide with the profile of an unknown Indian maiden painted on it, and the rocking-chair held a leather pillow bearing the picture, done by pyrography, of a girl in a fencing costume which set off her distressingly dated figure.

Mr. Durant's books were lined up behind the glass of the bookcase. They were all tall, thick books, brightly bound, and they justified his pride in their showing. They were mostly accounts of favorites of the French court, with a few volumes on odd personal habits of various monarchs, and the adventures of former Russian monks. Mrs. Durant, who never had time to get around to reading, regarded them with awe, and thought of her husband as one of the country's leading bibliophiles. There were books, too, in the living-room, but those she had inherited or been given. She had arranged a few on the living-room table; they looked as if they had been placed there by the Gideons.

Mr. Durant thought of himself as an indefatigable collector and an insatiable reader. But he was always disappointed in his books, after he had sent for them. They were never so good as the advertisements had led him to believe.

Into his den Mr. Durant preceded his wife, and faced her, still frowning. His calm was not shattered, but it was punctured. Something annoying always had to go and come up. Wouldn't you know?

"Now you know perfectly well, Fan, we can't have that dog around," he told her. He used the low voice reserved for underwear and bathroom articles and kindred shady topics. There was all the kindness in his tones that one has for a backward child, but a Gibraltar-like firmness was behind it. "You must be crazy to even think we could for a minute. Why, I wouldn't give a she-dog houseroom, not for any amount of money. It's disgusting, that's what it is."

"Well, but, Father——" began Mrs. Durant, her hands again going off into their convulsions.

"Disgusting," he repeated. "You have a female around, and you know what happens. All the males in the neighborhood will be running after her. First thing you know, she'd be having puppies— and the way they look after they've had them, and all! That would be nice for the children to see, wouldn't it? I should think you'd think of the children, Fan. No, sir, there'll be nothing like that around here, not while I know it. Disgusting!"

"But the children," she said. "They'll be just simply——"

"Now you just leave all that to me," he reassured her. "I told them the dog could stay, and I've never broken a promise yet, have I? Here's what I'll do—I'll wait till they're asleep, and then I'll just take this little dog and put it out. Then, in the morning, you can tell them it ran away during the night, see?"

She nodded. Her husband patted her shoulder, in its crapy-smelling black silk. His peace with the world was once more intact, restored by this simple solution of the little difficulty. Again his mind wrapped itself in the knowledge that everything was all fixed, all ready for a nice, fresh start. His arm was still about his wife's shoulder as they went on in to dinner.

A CERTAIN LADY

My friend, Mrs. Legion, is one of those few, as tradition numbers them, who are New Yorkers by birth. This gives her an appreciable edge on the parvenus who are Manhattanites only by migration. The Legions occupy an apartment on upper Riverside Drive, in a building called "The Emdor"—an apt and amicable blending of the name of the owner's wife, Emma, with that of his daughter, Doris. Thus, at one crack, are any possible hard feelings averted, and a happy literary effect achieved. "Isn't it a cute idea?" Mrs. Legion asks you, when she has explained the origin of the title. "Isn't it," you answer, without an interrogation point. And there you both are, ready to start all over again.

Shortly—oh, anywhere from seven to ten minutes—after she has met you, Mrs. Legion is supplying you with all the ground floor information as to why she lives on Riverside Drive, instead of Park Avenue. There is all the sun they get, and that big kitchen, and the superintendent is so obliging, and just look how convenient the busses are. Not for worlds, she promises you, would she dwell in any other section of the city. Yet, oddly enough—just about enough—she may be found frequently inspecting and pricing Park Avenue apartments, and hopefully calling up real estate agents to inquire if the rents in that part of town have taken a change for the better since her last inquiry.

Although she lives as far from Park Avenue as it is possible to do and still keep out of Jersey, Mrs. Legion is cozily conversant of all the comings and goings, or what have you, of the Avenue dwellers. Breathlessly she pursues the society notes in the daily papers; promptly on their days of publication she buys the magazines dealing with the activities of the socially elect. Only drop a hat, and she can give you anything you want to know in the way of dates, and maiden names,

33

and who married whom, and how they are getting along, if any. She employs nicknames, in referring to members of the favored few hundred, with an easy casualness that gives her remarks a truly homey flavor.

Naturally, it eats into her time to keep so admirably posted on these matters. And Mrs. Legion is pretty hard pressed for time. You might think, with her husband earning a cheery income, with Junior and Barbara safely in school, and a pleasant sufficiency of maids—two will do it nicely—around the apartment, that Mrs. Legion's life would follow the course made celebrated by the proverbial Riley; but the days are all too short for her to complete her business. She is always late for her appointments, rushing in a bit breathless, almost embarrassingly apologetic for those things that lack of time has forced her to leave undone. You simply must excuse the way she looks, but she didn't have a minute to get her hair waved, or, goodness, she must try to crowd in a manicure somehow, or for heaven's sake, remind her to stop at the baker's on her way home—she didn't have a second all morning. Her life is passed in an oddly imperceptible process known as "getting around" to things,—getting around to answer a letter, getting around to having her fur coat done over, getting around to having a talk with Junior's teacher.

And then, of course, there is all her shopping to do. Mrs. Legion's shopping has never yet reached a stage even approaching completion. Rarely a day passes that she must not visit the stores, if not to purchase, then to look around and get an idea or so. To look at her, you realize instantly that it must indeed take time and thought and research for her to assemble her costumes, to get them so faithfully like those worn by all other women of her circumstances. Mrs. Legion and her friends dress with the uniformity of the Tiller girls. Their hats are of the same shape and worn at the same angle, their coiffures meticulously alike, their dresses follow one another closely in material and design, their shoes are of the same last. Not until she has sedulously effaced all traces of individuality does Mrs. Legion feel that she is smart enough to appear in public.

Duties aside, Mrs. Legion must have her fun, being only human. Her good times consist in meeting her women friends almost daily, either at her house or at one of theirs, and having a real old-fashioned talk. Sometimes this is staged over the bridge table, sometimes over the Mah Jong tiles, sometimes a bit of silky and lacy sewing. The Legion school of conversationalists deals entirely with personalities, nor does it fear to probe deep into the intimate affairs of absent acquaintances. Detailed stories of miserable matrimony and racking separation, of lingering illness and agonizing childbirth and ancestral insanity, of heartbreak and poverty and desertion burble melodiously from the ladies' cool, smooth, expensively rouged lips.

The talk is interrupted by the serving of a lavish and imaginative tea, of which Mrs. Legion partakes generously. She is always going to begin dieting next Monday morning.

For her further diversion, there are literature and the drama. Mrs. Legion is by her own admission a great reader. She has long been a member of the circulating library contained in the stationer's nearest her. She is saved the wear and tear of selecting appropriate reading matter—there is the nicest girl there, who knows just the sort of thing she likes. Mrs. Legion can seldom tell you the title of a book she reads, and never the author's name, but she can always give you a pretty comprehensive résumé of the plot. She likes a book because there is the cutest girl in it, or the most attractive man, or because the author says the rawest things,—well, my dear, simply nothing is left to your imagination. And the lifting of any strain on the imagination is regarded, in the Legion circle, as the king of assets.

In the theatre, she likes best to patronize, even though she must wait weeks to obtain desirable seats, those exhibits which she euphemistically describes as "my dear, they say it's the most off-color thing you ever saw. I do hope the police don't stop it before we can get tickets." She does not care for drama of the drab, the every-day, or the underworld. As she says, she does love to see pretty clothes.

Sporadically, Mrs. Legion goes in for culture in a really big way, and signs up for a course of lectures on Flemish paintings or current events or interior decoration. The first lecture of the series is largely attended and faithfully quoted: along about the sixth or seventh, only the first row of gilt chairs is occupied. Mrs. Legion has looked on this world for some thirty-seven years, and she has not failed to draw conclusions. So clear are her views that she can dismiss any subject with a single sentence. Of politics, she says that Mrs. Coolidge is awfully sweet looking, and they say she is very popular in Washington. Of the unemployment situation, that these beggars you see in the streets all have big bank accounts and probably most of them own tenement buildings. Of married life, that she honestly believes that Fred Legion would eat steak every night if you'd give it to him. Of the race question, that these Swedes and Irish girls are so independent that she has half a mind to get a couple of darkie servants. Of art and belles lettres, that she wouldn't live in Greenwich Village if you gave her the place. Of motherhood, that it certainly is hard to know how to dress children when they're at that awkward age. Of the relation of the sexes, that it's terrible what women have to go through in this world.

My friend, Mrs. Legion. Heiress of the ages.

THE WONDERFUL OLD GENTLEMAN
A STORY PROVING THAT NO ONE CAN HATE
LIKE A CLOSE RELATIVE

IF THE BAINS had striven for years, they could have been no more successful in making their living-room into a small but admirably complete museum of objects suggesting strain, discomfort, or the tomb. Yet they had never even tried for the effect. Some of the articles that the room contained were wedding-presents; some had been put in from time to time as substitutes as their predecessors succumbed to age and wear; a few had been brought along by the Old Gentleman when he had come to make his home with the Bains some five years before.

It was curious how perfectly they all fitted into the general scheme. It was as if they had all been selected by a single enthusiast to whom time was but little object, so long as he could achieve the eventual result of transforming the Bain living-room into a home chamber of horrors, modified a bit for family use.

It was a high-ceilinged room, with heavy, dark old woodwork, that brought long and unavoidable thoughts of silver handles and weaving worms. The paper was the color of stale mustard. Its design, once a dashing affair of a darker tone splashed with twinkling gold, had faded into lines and smears that resolved themselves, before the eyes of the sensitive, into hordes of battered heads and tortured profiles, some eyeless, some with clotted gashes for mouths.

The furniture was dark and cumbersome and subject to painful creakings—sudden, sharp creaks that seemed to be wrung from its brave silence only when it could bear no more. A close, earthy smell came from its dulled tapestry cushions, and try as Mrs. Bain might, furry gray dust accumulated in the crevices.

The center-table was upheld by the perpetually strained arms of three carved figures, insistently female to the waist, then trailing discreetly off into a confusion of scrolls and scales. Upon it rested a row of blameless books, kept in place at the ends by the straining shoulder-muscles of two bronze-colored plaster elephants, forever pushing at their tedious toil.

On the heavily carved mantel was a gayly colored figure of a curly-headed peasant boy, ingeniously made so that he sat on the shelf and dangled one leg over. He was in the eternal act of removing a thorn from his chubby foot, his round face realistically wrinkled with the cruel pain. Just above him hung a steel-engraving of a chariot-race, the dust flying, the chariots careening wildly, the drivers ferociously lashing their maddened horses, the horses themselves caught by the artist the moment before their hearts burst, and they dropped in their traces.

The opposite wall was devoted to the religious in art; a steel-engraving of the Crucifixion, lavish of ghastly detail; a sepia-print of the martyrdom of Saint Sebastian, the cords cutting deep into the arms writhing from the stake, arrows bristling in the thick, soft-looking body; a water-color copy of a "Mother of Sorrows," the agonized eyes raised to a cold heaven, great, bitter tears forever on the wan cheeks, paler for the grave-like draperies that wrapped the head.

Beneath the windows hung a painting in oil of two lost sheep, huddled hopelessly together in the midst of a wild blizzard. This was one of the Old Gentleman's contributions to the room. Mrs. Bain was wont to observe of it that the frame was worth she didn't know how much.

The wall-space beside the door was reserved for a bit of modern art that had once caught Mr. Bain's eye in a stationer's window—a colored print, showing a railroad-crossing, with a train flying relentlessly toward it, and a low, red automobile trying to dash across the track before the iron terror shattered it into eternity. Nervous visitors who were given chairs facing this scene usually made opportunity to change their seats before they could give their whole minds to the conversation.

The ornaments, placed with careful casualness on the table and the upright piano, included a small gilt lion of Lucerne, a little, chipped, plaster Laocoön, and a savage china kitten eternally about to pounce upon a plump and helpless china mouse. This last had been one of the Old Gentleman's own wedding-gifts. Mrs. Bain explained, in tones low with awe, that it was very old.

The ash-receivers, of Oriental manufacture, were in the form of grotesque heads, tufted with bits of gray human hair, and given bulging, dead, glassy eyes and mouths stretched into great gapes, into which those who had the heart for it might flick their ashes. Thus the smallest details of the room kept loyally to the spirit of the thing, and carried on the effect.

But the three people now sitting in the Bains' living-room were not in the least oppressed by the decorative scheme. Two of them, Mr. and Mrs. Bain, not only had had twenty-eight years of the room to accustom themselves to it, but had been stanch admirers of it from the first. And no surroundings, however morbid, could close in on the aristocratic calm of Mrs. Bain's sister, Mrs. Whittaker.

She graciously patronized the very chair she now sat in, smiled kindly on the glass of cider she held in her hand. The Bains were poor, and Mrs. Whittaker had, as it is ingenuously called, married well, and none of them ever lost sight of these facts.

But Mrs. Whittaker's attitude of kindly tolerance was not confined to her less fortunate relatives. It extended to friends of her youth, working people, the arts, politics, the United States in general, and God, Who had always supplied her with the best of service. She could have given Him an excellent reference at any time.

The three people sat with a comfortable look of spending the evening. There was an air of expectancy about them, a not unpleasant little nervousness, as of those who wait for a curtain to rise. Mrs. Bain had brought in cider in the best tumblers, and had served some of her nut cookies in the plate painted by hand with clusters of cherries— the plate she had used for sandwiches when, several years ago, her card club had met at her house.

She had thought it over a little tonight, before she lifted out the cherry plate, then quickly decided and resolutely heaped it with cookies. After all, it was an occasion—informal, perhaps, but still an occasion. The Old Gentleman was dying upstairs. At five o'clock that afternoon the doctor had said that it would be a surprise to him if the Old Gentleman lasted till the middle of the night—a big surprise, he had augmented.

There was no need for them to gather at the Old Gentleman's bedside. He would not have known any of them. In fact, he had not known them for almost a year, addressing them by wrong names and asking them grave, courteous questions about the health of husbands or wives or children who belonged to other branches of the family. And he was quite unconscious now.

Miss Chester, the nurse who had been with him since "this last stroke," as Mrs. Bain importantly called it, was entirely competent to attend and watch him. She had promised to call them if, in her tactful words, she saw any signs.

So the Old Gentleman's daughters and son-in-law waited in the warm living-room, and sipped their cider, and conversed in low, polite tones.

Mrs. Bain cried a little in pauses in the conversation. She had always cried easily and often. Yet, in spite of her years of practice, she did not do it well. Her eyelids grew pink and sticky, and her nose gave her no little trouble, necessitating almost constant sniffling. She sniffled loudly and conscientiously, and frequently removed her pince-nez to wipe her eyes with a crumpled handkerchief, gray with damp.

Mrs. Whittaker, too, bore a handkerchief, but she appeared to be holding it in waiting. She was dressed, in compliment to the occasion, in her black crepe de Chine, and she had left her lapis-lazuli pin, her olivine bracelet, and her topaz and amethyst rings at home in her bureau drawer, retaining only her lorgnette on its gold chain, in case there should be any reading to be done.

Mrs. Whittaker's dress was always studiously suited to its occasion; thus, her bearing had always that calm that only the correctly attired may enjoy. She was an authority on where to place monograms on linen, how to instruct working folk, and what to say in letters of condolence. The word "lady" figured largely in her conversation. Blood, she often predicted, would tell.

Mrs. Bain wore a rumpled white shirt-waist and the old blue skirt she saved for "around the kitchen." There had been time to change, after she had telephoned the doctor's verdict to her sister, but she had not been quite sure whether it was the thing to do. She had thought that Mrs. Whittaker might expect her to display a little distraught untidiness at a time like this; might even go in for it in a mild way herself.

Now Mrs. Bain looked at her sister's elaborately curled, painstakingly brown coiffure, and nervously patted her own straggling hair, gray at the front, with strands of almost lime-color in the little twist at the back. Her eyelids grew wet and sticky again, and she hung her glasses over one forefinger while she applied the damp handkerchief. After all, she reminded herself and the others, it was her poor father.

Oh, but it was really the best thing, Mrs. Whittaker explained in her gentle, patient voice.

"You wouldn't want to see Father go on like this," she pointed out. Mr. Bain echoed her, as if struck with the idea. Mrs. Bain had nothing to reply to them. No, she wouldn't want to see the Old Gentleman go on like this.

Five years before, Mrs. Whittaker had decided that the Old Gentleman was getting too old to live alone with only old Annie to cook for him and look after him. It was only a question of a little time before it "wouldn't have looked right," his living alone, when he had his children to take care of him. Mrs. Whittaker always stopped things before they got to the stage where they didn't look right. So he had come to live with the Bains.

Some of his furniture had been sold; a few things, such as his silver, his tall clock, and the Persian rug he had bought at the Exposition, Mrs. Whittaker had found room for in her own house; and some he brought with him to the Bains'.

Mrs. Whittaker's house was much larger than her sister's, and she had three servants and no children. But, as she told her friends, she had held back and let Allie and Lewis have the Old Gentleman.

"You see," she explained, dropping her voice to the tones reserved for not very pretty subjects, "Allie and Lewis are—well, they haven't a great deal."

So it was gathered that the Old Gentleman would do big things for the Bains when he came to live with them. Not exactly by paying board—it is a little too much to ask your father to pay for his food and lodging, as if he were a stranger. But, as Mrs. Whittaker suggested, he could do a great deal in the way of buying needed things for the house and keeping everything going.

And the Old Gentleman did contribute to the Bain household. He bought an electric heater and an electric fan, new curtains, storm-windows, and light-fixtures, all for his bedroom; and had a nice little bathroom for his personal use made out of the small guest-room adjoining it.

He shopped for days until he found a coffee-cup large enough for his taste; he bought several large ash-trays, and a dozen extra-size bath-towels, that Mrs. Bain marked with his initials. And every Christmas and birthday he gave Mrs. Bain a round, new, shining ten-dollar gold piece. Of course, he presented gold pieces to Mrs. Whittaker, too, on like appropriate occasions. The Old Gentleman prided himself always on his fair-mindedness. He often said that he was not one to show any favoritism.

Mrs. Whittaker was Cordelia-like to her father during his declining years. She came to see him several times a month, bringing him jelly or potted hyacinths. Sometimes she sent her car and chauffeur for him, so that he might take an easy drive through the town, and Mrs. Bain might be afforded a chance to drop her cooking and accompany him. When Mrs. Whittaker was away on trips with her husband, she almost never neglected to send her father picture post-cards of various points of interest.

The Old Gentleman appreciated her affection, and took pride in her. He enjoyed being told that she was like him.

"That Hattie," he used to tell Mrs. Bain, "she's a fine woman—a fine woman."

As soon as she had heard that the Old Gentleman was dying Mrs. Whittaker had come right over, stopping only to change her dress and have her dinner. Her husband was away in the woods with some men, fishing. She explained to the Bains that there was no use in disturbing him—it would have been impossible for him to get back that night. As soon as—well, if anything happened she would telegraph him, and he could return in time for the funeral.

Mrs. Bain was sorry that he was away. She liked her ruddy, jovial, loud-voiced brother-in-law.

"It's too bad that Clint couldn't be here," she said, as she had said several times before. "He's so fond of cider," she added.

"Father," said Mrs. Whittaker, "was always very fond of Clint." Already the Old Gentleman had slipped into the past tense.

"Everybody likes Clint," Mr. Bain stated.

He was included in the "everybody." The last time he had failed in business, Clint had given him the clerical position he had since held over at the brush works. It was pretty generally understood that this had been brought about through Mrs. Whittaker's intervention, but still they were Clint's brush works, and it was Clint who paid him his salary. And forty dollars a week is indubitably forty dollars a week.

"I hope he'll be sure and be here in time for the funeral," said Mrs. Bain. "It will be Wednesday morning, I suppose, Hat?"

Mrs. Whittaker nodded.

"Or perhaps around two o'clock Wednesday afternoon," she amended. "I always think that's a nice time. Father has his frock coat, Allie?"

"Oh, yes," Mrs. Bain said eagerly. "And it's all clean and lovely. He has everything. Hattie, I noticed the other day at Mr. Newton's funeral they had more of a blue necktie on him, so I suppose they're wearing them—Mollie Newton always has everything just so. But I don't know——"

"I think," said Mrs. Whittaker firmly, "that there is nothing lovelier than black for an old gentleman."

"Poor Old Gentleman," said Mr. Bain, shaking his head. "He would have been eighty-five if he just could have lived till next September. Well, I suppose it's all for the best."

He took a small draft of cider and another cooky.

"A wonderful, wonderful life," summarized Mrs. Whittaker. "And a wonderful, wonderful old gentleman."

"Well, I should say so," said Mrs. Bain. "Why, up to the last year he was as interested in everything! It was, 'Allie, how much do you have to give for your eggs now?' and 'Allie, why don't you change your butcher?—this one's robbing you,' and 'Allie, who was that you were talking to on the telephone?' all day long! Everybody used to speak of it."

"And he used to come to the table right up to this stroke," Mr. Bain related, chuckling reminiscently. "My, he used to raise Cain when Allie didn't cut up his meat fast enough to suit him. Always had a temper, *I'll* tell you, the Old Gentleman did. Wouldn't stand for us having anybody in to meals—he didn't like that worth a cent. Eighty-four years old, and sitting right up there at the table with us!"

They vied in telling instances of the Old Gentleman's intelligence and liveliness, as parents cap one another's anecdotes of precocious children.

"It's only the past year that he had to be helped up- and downstairs," said Mrs. Bain. "Walked up-stairs all by himself, and more than eighty years old!"

Mrs. Whittaker was amused.

"I remember you said that once when Clint was here," she remarked, "and Clint said, 'Well, if you can't walk up-stairs by the time you're eighty, when are you going to learn?'"

Mrs. Bain smiled politely, because her brother-in-law had said it. Otherwise she would have been shocked and wounded.

"Yes, sir," said Mr. Bain. "Wonderful."

"The only thing I could have wished," Mrs. Bain said, after a pause—"I could have wished he'd been a little different about Paul. Somehow I've never felt quite right since Paul went into the navy."

Mrs. Whittaker's voice fell into the key used for the subject that has been gone over and over and over again.

"Now, Allie," she said, "you know yourself that was the best thing that could have happened. Father told you that himself, often and often. Paul was young, and he wanted to have all his young friends running in and out of the house, banging doors and making all sorts of racket, and it would have been a terrible nuisance for father. You must realize that father was more than eighty years old, Allie."

"Yes, I know," Mrs. Bain said. Her eyes went to the photograph of her son in his seaman's uniform, and she sighed.

"And besides," Mrs. Whittaker pointed out triumphantly, "now that Miss Chester's here in Paul's room, there wouldn't have been any room for him. So you see!"

There was rather a long pause. Then Mrs. Bain edged toward the other thing that had been weighing upon her.

"Hattie," she said, "I suppose—I suppose we'd ought to let Matt know?"

"I shouldn't," said Mrs. Whittaker composedly. She always took great pains with her "shall's" and "will's." "I only hope that he doesn't see it in the papers in time to come on for the funeral. If you want to have your brother turn up drunk at the services, Allie, *I* don't."

"But I thought he'd straightened up," said Mr. Bain. "Thought he was all right since he got married."

"Yes, I know, I know, Lewis," Mrs. Whittaker said wearily. "I've heard all about that. All I say is, *I* know what Matt is."

"John Loomis was telling me," reported Mr. Bain, "he was going through Akron, and he stopped off to see Matt. Said they had a nice little place, and he seemed to be getting along fine. Said she seemed like a cracker-jack housekeeper."

Mrs. Whittaker smiled.

"Yes," she said, "John Loomis and Matt were always two of a kind—you couldn't believe a word either of them said. Probably she did seem to be a good housekeeper. I've no doubt she acted the part very well. Matt never made any bones of the fact that she was on the stage once, for almost a year. Excuse me from having that woman come to Father's funeral. If you want to know what *I* think, *I* think that Matt marrying a woman like that had a good deal to do with hastening Father's death."

The Bains sat in awe.

"And after all Father did for Matt, too," added Mrs. Whittaker, her voice shaken.

"Well, I should think so," Mr. Bain was glad to agree. "I remember how the Old Gentleman used to try and help Matt get along. He'd go down, like it was to Mr. Fuller, that time Matt was working at the bank, and he'd explain to him, 'Now, Mr. Fuller,' he'd say, 'I don't know whether you know it, but this son of mine has always been what you might call the black sheep of the family. He's been kind of a drinker,' he'd say, 'and he's got himself into trouble a couple of times, and if you'd just keep an eye on him, so's to see he keeps straight, it'd be a favor to me.'

"Mr. Fuller told me about it himself. Said it was wonderful the way the Old Gentleman came right out and talked just as frankly to him. Said *he'd* never had any idea Matt was that way—wanted to hear all about it."

Mrs. Whittaker nodded sadly.

"Oh, I know," she said. "Time and again Father would do that. And then, as like as not, Matt would get one of his sulky fits, and not turn up at his work."

"And when Matt would be out of work," Mrs. Bain said, "the way Father'd hand him out his car-fare, and I don't know what all! When Matt was a grown man, going on thirty years old, Father would take him down to Newins & Malley's and buy him a whole new outfit—pick out everything himself. He always used to say Matt was the kind that would get cheated out of his eye-teeth if he went into a store alone."

"My, Father hated to see anybody make a fool of themselves about money," Mrs. Whittaker commented. "Remember how he always used to say, 'Anybody can make money, but it takes a wise man to keep it'?"

"I suppose he must be a pretty rich man," Mr. Bain said, abruptly restoring the Old Gentleman to the present.

"Oh—rich!" Mrs. Whittaker's smile was at its kindliest. "But he managed his affairs very well, Father did, right up to the last. Everything is in splendid shape, Clint says."

"He showed you the will, didn't he, Hat?" asked Mrs. Bain, forming bits of her sleeve into little plaits between her thin, hard fingers.

"Yes," said her sister. "Yes, he did. He showed me the will. A little over a year ago, I think it was, wasn't it? You know, just before he started to fail, that time."

She took a small bite of cooky.

"*Awfully* good," she said. She broke into a little bubbly laugh, the laugh she used at teas and wedding receptions and fairly formal dinners. "You know," she went on, as one sharing a good story, "he's gone and left all that old money to me. 'Why, Father!' I said, as soon as I'd read that part. But it seems he'd gotten some sort of idea in his head that Clint and I would be able to take care of it better than anybody else, and you know what Father was, once he made up that mind of his. You can just imagine how *I* felt. I couldn't say a thing."

She laughed again, shaking her head in amused bewilderment.

"Oh, and Allie," she said, "he's left you all the furniture he brought here with him, and all the things he bought since he came. And Lewis is to have his set of Thackeray. And that money he lent Lewis, to try and tide him over in the hardware business that time—that's to be regarded as a gift."

She sat back and looked at them, smiling.

"Lewis paid back most all of that money Father lent him that time," Mrs. Bain said. "There was only about two hundred dollars more, and then he would have had it all paid up."

"That's to be regarded as a gift," insisted Mrs. Whittaker. She leaned over and patted her brother-in-law's arm. "Father always liked you, Lewis," she said softly.

"Poor Old Gentleman," murmured Mr. Bain.

"Did it—did it say anything about Matt?" asked Mrs. Bain.

"Oh, Allie!" Mrs. Whittaker gently reproved her. "When you think of all the money Father spent and spent on Matt, it seems to me he did more than enough—more than enough. And then when Matt went way off there to live, and married that woman, and never a word about it—Father hearing it all through strangers—well, I don't think any of us realize how it hurt Father. He never said much about it, but I don't think he ever got over it. I'm always so thankful that poor dear mother didn't live to see how Matt turned out."

"Poor Mother," said Mrs. Bain shakily, and brought the grayish handkerchief into action once more. "I can hear her now, just as plain. 'Now, children,' she used to say, 'do for goodness' sake let's all try and keep your father in a good humor.' If I've heard her say it once, I've heard her say it a hundred times. Remember, Hat?"

"Do I remember!" said Mrs. Whittaker. "And do you remember how they used to play whist, and how furious Father used to get when he lost?"

"Yes," Mrs. Bain cried excitedly, "and how Mother used to have to cheat, so as to be sure and not win from him? She got so she used to be able to do it just as well!"

They laughed softly, filled with memories of the gone days. A pleasant, thoughtful silence fell around them.

Mrs. Bain patted a yawn to extinction, and looked at the clock.

"Ten minutes to eleven," she said. "Goodness, I had no idea it was anywhere near so late. I wish—" She stopped just in time, crimson at what her wish would have been.

"You see, Lew and I have got in the way of going to bed early," she explained. "Father slept so light, we couldn't have people in like we used to before he came here, to play a little bridge or anything, on account of disturbing him. And if we wanted to go to the movies or anywhere, he'd go on so about being left alone that we just kind of gave up going."

"Oh, the Old Gentleman always let you know what he wanted," said Mr. Bain, smiling. "He was a wonder, *I'll* tell you. Nearly eighty-five years old!"

"Think of it," said Mrs. Whittaker.

A door clicked open above them, and feet ran quickly and not lightly down the stairs. Miss Chester burst into the room.

"Oh, Mrs. Bain!" she cried. "Oh, the Old Gentleman! Oh, he's gone! I noticed him kind of stirring and whimpering a little, and he seemed to be trying to make motions at his warm milk, like as if he wanted some. So I put the cup up to his mouth, and he sort of fell over, and just like that he was gone, and the milk all over him."

Mrs. Bain instantly collapsed into passionate weeping. Her husband put his arm tenderly about her, and murmured a series of "Now-now's."

Mrs. Whittaker rose, set her cider-glass carefully on the table, shook out her handkerchief, and moved toward the door.

"A lovely death," she pronounced. "A wonderful, wonderful life, and now a beautiful, peaceful death. Oh, it's the best thing, Allie; it's the best thing."

"Oh, it is, Mrs. Bain; it's the best thing," Miss Chester said earnestly. "It's really a blessing. That's what it is."

Among them they got Mrs. Bain up the stairs.

DIALOGUE AT THREE IN THE MORNING

"Plain water in mine," said the woman in the petunia-colored hat. "Or never mind about the water. Hell with it. Just straight Scotch. What I care? Just straight. That's me. Never gave anybody any trouble in my life. All right, they can say what they like about me, but I know—I know—I never gave anybody any trouble in my life. You can tell them that from me, see? What I care?"

"Listen," said the man with the ice-blue hair. And he leaned across the table toward her, and frowned heavily at the designs he drew with the plated knife. "Listen. I just want you to get this thing clear——"

"Yeah," she said. "Get things clear. That's good. That gives me a big laugh. That's laughable, a thing like that is. Say, if there's anybody around here that's going to get things clear, I'm going to be the one around here that's going to get things clear. What you do, you go back to Jeannette, see, and you tell her I know what she's saying about me. I don't want to get you into this, but you tell her that from me. You can keep out of it. You don't have to tell her you told me. You don't even have to tell her you saw me. Say, if you're ashamed to tell people you know me, that's all right with me, see? I'm not going to give anybody any trouble. If you're ashamed to tell your friends you're a friend of mine, what I care? I guess I'll be able to stand that, all right. I've stood a lot of things."

"Ah, listen," he said. "Listen. Will you please listen just a minute?"

"Yeah, listen," she said. "That's fine. Listen. Well, I'm through with this listening stuff. You can tell them all from me, see, I'm going to be the one that's going to do the talking from now on. You can tell Jeannette that. What I care? You can run right to her and blab that. Says I look fat in my red dress, does she? That's a nice thing to

48

have anybody say about you. Makes you feel great, that does. You can tell Miss Jeannette she's got a lot to do to make cracks about a person's red dress. That's pretty laughable, that is. Say, when I ask her to pay for anything I wear, then it will be time for her to crack. Her or anybody else. I make my own living, thank God, and I don't have to ask anybody for anything. You can tell them all that. You or anybody else."

"Will you do me a favor?" he said. "Will you do me one little favor? Will you? Will you listen just———"

"Yeah, favors," she said. "Nobody's got to do me any favors. I make my own living, and I don't have to ask any favors off of anybody. I never gave anybody any trouble in my life. And if they don't like it, they know what they can do. Tiffany's window, see? The whole lot of them. Oh, did I break that glass? Oh, isn't that terrible. All right—if it's broken it's broken. Isn't it? Hell with it. Hell with them all."

"If you'd listen," he said. "There isn't anything for you to get sore about. Just listen———"

"Who's sore?" she said. "I'm not sore. I'm all right. You don't have to worry about me. You or Jeannette or anybody else. Sore. Say, if a person's not going to get sore about a thing like that, what kind of a thing is a person expected to get sore about? After all I've done for her. Trouble with me is, I'm too kind-hearted. That's what everybody always told me. 'Trouble with you is, you're too kind-hearted,' they said. And now look what she goes around and says about me. And you let her say a thing like that to you, and you're ashamed to say you're a friend of mine. All right, you don't have to. You can go back to Jeannette and stay there. The whole lot of you."

"Now listen, sweetheart," he said. "Haven't I always been your friend? Haven't I? Well now, wouldn't you listen to your friend just for a———"

"Friends," she said. "Friends. Fine lot of friends I got. Go around cutting your throat. That's what you get for being kind-hearted. Just a big kind-hearted slob. That's me. Oh, hell with the water. I'll drink it straight. I make my own living, and go around not giving anybody any trouble, and then the whole lot of them turn on me. After the way I was brought up, and the home we used to have, and all, and they go around making cracks about me. Work all day long, and don't ask anything off of anybody. And here I am with a weak heart, besides. I'd just as soon I was dead. What've I got to live for, anyway? Kindly answer me that one question. What've I got to live for?"

Tears striped her cheeks.

The man with the ice-blue hair reached across the Scotch-soaked tablecloth and took her hand.

"Ah, listen," he said. "Listen."

From the unknown, a waiter appeared. He chirped and fluttered about them. Presently, you felt, he would cover them with leaves. . . .

THE LAST TEA

THE YOUNG MAN in the chocolate-brown suit sat down at the table, where the girl with the artificial camellia had been sitting for forty minutes.

"Guess I must be late," he said. "Sorry you been waiting."

"Oh, goodness!" she said. "I just got here myself, just about a second ago. I simply went ahead and ordered because I was dying for a cup of tea. I was late, myself. I haven't been here more than a minute."

"That's good," he said. "Hey, hey, easy on the sugar—one lump is fair enough. And take away those cakes. Terrible! Do I feel terrible!"

"Ah," she said, "you do? Ah. Whadda matter?"

"Oh, I'm ruined," he said. "I'm in terrible shape."

"Ah, the poor boy," she said. "Was it feelin' mizzable? Ah, and it came way up here to meet me! You shouldn't have done that—I'd have understood. Ah, just think of it coming all the way up here when it's so sick!"

"Oh, that's all right," he said. "I might as well be here as any place else. Any place is like any other place, the way I feel today. Oh, I'm all shot."

"Why, that's just awful," she said. "Why, you poor sick thing. Goodness, I hope it isn't influenza. They say there's a lot of it around."

"Influenza!" he said. "I wish that was all I had. Oh, I'm poisoned. I'm through. I'm off the stuff for life. Know what time I got to bed? Twenty minutes past five, A.M., this morning. What a night! What an evening!"

"I thought," she said, "that you were going to stay at the office and work late. You said you'd be working every night this week."

"Yeah, I know," he said. "But it gave me the jumps, thinking about going down there and sitting at that desk. I went up to May's—

51

she was throwing a party. Say, there was somebody there said they knew you."

"Honestly?" she said. "Man or woman?"

"Dame," he said. "Name's Carol McCall. Say, why haven't I been told about her before? That's what I call a girl. What a looker she is!"

"Oh, really?" she said. "That's funny—I never heard of anyone that thought that. I've heard people say she was sort of nice-looking, if she wouldn't make up so much. But I never heard of anyone that thought she was pretty."

"Pretty is right," he said. "What a couple of eyes she's got on her!"

"Really?" she said. "I never noticed them particularly. But I haven't seen her for a long time—sometimes people change, or something."

"She says she used to go to school with you," he said.

"Well, we went to the same school," she said. "I simply happened to go to public school because it happened to be right near us, and Mother hated to have me crossing streets. But she was three or four classes ahead of me. She's ages older than I am."

"She's three or four classes ahead of them all," he said. "Dance! Can she step! 'Burn your clothes, baby,' I kept telling her. I must have been fried pretty."

"I was out dancing myself, last night," she said. "Wally Dillon and I. He's just been pestering me to go out with him. He's the most wonderful dancer. Goodness! I didn't get home till I don't know what time. I must look just simply a wreck. Don't I?"

"You look all right," he said.

"Wally's crazy," she said. "The things he says! For some crazy reason or other, he's got it into his head that I've got beautiful eyes, and, well, he just kept talking about them till I didn't know where to look, I was so embarrassed. I got so red, I thought everybody in the place would be looking at me. I got just as red as a brick. Beautiful eyes! Isn't he crazy?"

"He's all right," he said. "Say, this little McCall girl, she's had all kinds of offers to go into moving pictures. 'Why don't you go ahead and go?' I told her. But she says she doesn't feel like it."

"There was a man up at the lake, two summers ago," she said. "He was a director or something with one of the big moving-picture people—oh, he had all kinds of influence!—and he used to keep insisting and insisting that I ought to be in the movies. Said I ought to be doing sort of Garbo parts. I used to just laugh at him. Imagine!"

"She's had about a million offers," he said. "I told her to go ahead and go. She keeps getting these offers all the time."

"Oh, really?" she said. "Oh, listen, I knew I had something to ask you. Did you call me up last night, by any chance?"

"Me?" he said. "No, I didn't call you."

"While I was out, Mother said this man's voice kept calling up," she said. "I thought maybe it might be you, by some chance. I wonder who it could have been. Oh—I guess I know who it was. Yes, that's who it was!"

"No, I didn't call you," he said. "I couldn't have seen a telephone, last night. What a head I had on me, this morning! I called Carol up, around ten, and she said she was feeling great. Can that girl hold her liquor!"

"It's a funny thing about me," she said. "It just makes me feel sort of sick to see a girl drink. It's just something in me, I guess. I don't mind a man so much, but it makes me feel perfectly terrible to see a girl get intoxicated. It's just the way I am, I suppose."

"Does she carry it!" he said. "And then feels great the next day. There's a girl! Hey, what are you doing there? I don't want any more tea, thanks. I'm not one of these tea boys. And these tea rooms give me the jumps. Look at all those old dames, will you? Enough to give you the jumps."

"Of course, if you'd rather be some place, drinking, with I don't know what kinds of people," she said, "I'm sure I don't see how I can help that. Goodness, there are enough people that are glad enough to take me to tea. I don't know how many people keep calling me up and pestering me to take me to tea. Plenty of people!"

"All right, all right, I'm here, aren't I?" he said. "Keep your hair on."

"I could name them all day," she said.

"All right," he said. "What's there to crab about?"

"Goodness, it isn't any of my business what you do," she said. "But I hate to see you wasting your time with people that aren't nearly good enough for you. That's all."

"No need worrying over me," he said. "I'll be all right. Listen. You don't have to worry."

"It's just I don't like to see you wasting your time," she said, "staying up all night and then feeling terribly the next day. Ah, I was forgetting he was so sick. Ah, I was mean, wasn't I, scolding him when he was so mizzable. Poor boy. How's he feel now?"

"Oh, I'm all right," he said, "I feel fine. You want anything else? How about getting a check? I got to make a telephone call before six."

"Oh, really?" she said. "Calling up Carol?"

"She said she might be in around now," he said.

"Seeing her tonight?" she said.

"She's going to let me know when I call up," he said. "She's probably got about a million dates. Why?"

"I was just wondering," she said. "Goodness, I've got to fly! I'm having dinner with Wally, and he's so crazy, he's probably there now. He's called me up about a hundred times today."

"Wait till I pay the check," he said, "and I'll put you on a bus."

"Oh, don't bother," she said. "It's right at the corner. I've got to fly. I suppose you want to stay and call up your friend from here?"

"It's an idea," he said. "Sure you'll be all right?"

OH! HE'S CHARMING!

"MR. PAWLING," SAID the hostess, "this is a great admirer of your books. Miss Waldron, Mr. Pawling. Miss Waldron, oh, she's a great admirer of yours."

She laughed heartily and highly, and melted away through the crowd, toward the depleted tea-table. Her lips were scrolled in sunshine, but in her eyes was the look of the caged thing, the look of the tortured soul who is wondering what in hell has become of that fresh supply of toast.

"Want to sit down?" said the author. "Here's a couple of chairs. Might as well grab them."

"Ooh, let's!" said the great admirer. "Let's do!"

So they did.

"God, I'm tired," said the author. "Dead, I am. Terrible party, this is. Terrible people. Everybody here's terrible. Lot of lice."

"Oh, you must get so sick of parties!" said the great admirer. "You must be simply bored to death. I suppose people are after you every second with invitations."

"I never answer them," he said. "I won't even go to the telephone any more. But they get you, anyhow. Look at me now. Stuck."

"Oh, it must be simply terrible," she said. "I was thinking, when I was watching you, before. Everybody crowding around you every minute."

"What's a person going to do?" he said.

"No, but really," she said, "you can't blame them, you know. Naturally everybody wants to meet you. My heavens, I've been just simply dying to, ever since I read *Some Ladies in Agony*. I just love every word of that book. I've read it over and over. But my heavens, I suppose so many people tell you how they love your books, it would simply bore you to death to hear me rave about them."

55

"Not at all," he said. "That's quite all right."

"Oh, I do," she said. "I love them. I've often thought 'I'd just love to sit down and write Freeman Pawling a little letter.' But I couldn't get up the nerve to. I was simply scared to death of you. Do you mind if I say something awfully personal? I had no idea you'd be so young!"

"That so?" he said.

"Why, I thought you'd have gray hair, at least," she said. "I thought anybody would have to be old, to know as much as you do."

"That so?" he said.

"My heavens," she said, "the things you know! Why, I thought nobody but me knew them. Do you mind if I ask you an awfully personal question? How on earth did you ever find out so much about women?"

"Oh, my God," he said, "I've known a million of them. All over the world."

"You don't have to tell me," she said. "I bet you have. I bet you've left broken hearts wherever you've gone. Haven't you?"

"Well," he said.

"It must be just simply awful for any woman you know," she said. "The way you see right through and through them. I'd better be terribly careful what I say. First thing I know, you'll be putting me in a book. Look, I'm going to ask you something awfully personal. Do you mind? Look, was Cicely Celtic in *Various Knights and a Lady* drawn from real life?"

"She was," he said, "and she wasn't. Partly she was, and partly she wasn't."

"That's what I thought," she said.

"She was rather an amusing little thing," he said, "the real Cicely. Girl named Nancy James—very good family. A lady. Possessive as the devil, though. She's dead, now. Shot herself."

"Ooh," she said. "Just like in the book!"

"Yes," he said. "I thought I might as well use it. After all the trouble she was. God, what a jealous little ape."

"Are you writing anything now?" she said.

"Oh, it's coming slowly," he said. "Coming slowly. It doesn't do to hurry it."

"I was in at the library yesterday," she said. "Isn't it funny, I was just asking them if you had anything new out, and they said no. They said no, you didn't. I always ask them what's good, and they sort of save out books for me. I got a lot. There's one of them by Sherwood Anderson. The *Dark* something, or something."

"Don't read it," he said. "It's a louse. Poor Anderson's all through."

"Oh, I'm awfully glad you told me," she said. "Now I won't have to waste my time over it. Then I got this Dreiser thing, only it's in two books, and it looks terribly long."

"Dreiser trying to write," he said. "That's one of the funniest things in the world. He can't write."

"Well, I'm glad to know that," she said. "I won't have to bother with it. Let's see—oh, I got this new Ring Lardner book. Short stories or something."

"Who?" he said.

"You know," she said. "He used to write funny things. You know, all those funny things. Everything spelled wrong, and everything."

"What's his name?" he said.

"Lardner," she said. "Ring Lardner. It's a funny name, isn't it?"

"It's a new one on me," he said.

"Well, I really just got it mostly for Daddy," she said. "He's crazy about baseball and things. I thought he'd probably be crazy about it. I just can't seem to find any books I like, any more. My heavens, I wish you'd hurry up and finish your new one. I wish I had the nerve to ask you something awfully personal. I wonder if you'd mind. What's your new book like?"

"It's different," he said. "Entirely different. I have evolved a different form. The trouble with novelists is their form. It's their form, if you see what I mean. In this book, I have taken an entirely different form: It's evolved from the *Satyricon* of Petronius."

"Ooh," she said. "Ooh. Exciting!"

"A good deal of the scene," he said, "is laid in Egypt. I think they're about ready for it."

"How gorgeous!" she said. "I simply love anything about Egypt. I'm just crazy to go there. Have you ever been?"

"No," he said. "I'm sick of traveling. It's the same thing everywhere. People giving parties. Terrible."

"Oh, I know," she said. "It must be awful. Look, I don't want you to think I'm being awfully personal, but I was just thinking I'd simply love to have you come up to the house for tea some time. I wonder if you would."

"God, I'm through for the year," he said. "This is the last time they get me out."

"But just quietly," she said. "Just a few people that are crazy about your things, too. Or just nobody, if you like."

"For God's sake, when would I have any time?" he said.

"Well, just in case you ever do," she said, "it's in the telephone book. D. G. Waldron. Do you think you can remember that or shall I write it down?"

"Don't write it," he said. "I never carry women's addresses around with me. It's hot as hell in here. I'm going to duck. Well, good-bye."

"Oh, are you going?" she said. "Well, good-bye, then. I can't tell you how exciting it's been, meeting you and all. I hope to goodness I haven't bored you to death, raving about your books. But if you knew how I read them and read them! I simply can't wait to tell everybody I've really met Freeman Pawling!"

"Not at all," he said.

"And any time you're not just terribly busy," she said, "it's in the telephone book. You know!"

"Well, good-bye," he said.

He was out the door in eight seconds flat, with no time out for farewells to his hostess.

The great admirer crossed the room to the tea-table, and clutched the hostess by her weary and flaccid hand.

"Oh, my dear," she said, "it was just simply too thrilling for anything. Oh, he's charming!"

"Isn't he?" said the hostess. "I knew you'd think so, too."

TRAVELOGUE

THE WOMAN IN the spangled black dress left the rest of the party, and made room on the sofa for the sunburned young man with the quiet eyes.

"You just sit yourself right down here this minute," she said. "And give an account of yourself. The idea! Running away for nearly two years, and not even a post-card out of you! Aren't you ashamed? Answer Muvver. Izzun you tebble shame you'self?"

"I'm rotten about writing letters," he said. "I'm sorry. I guess I'm hopeless. I always mean to write, and I never seem to get around to it. It isn't because I don't think of people. It's just I'm terrible about writing letters."

"Where have you been, anyway?" she said. "Nearly two years! Where dat bad boy been teepin' himself?"

"Well, I was in Arabia, mostly," he said.

"You're crazy," she said. "Just simply crazy. What on earth did you want to go to a place like that for?"

"I don't know," he said. "I just sort of thought I'd like to see it."

"Oh, I know," she said. "You don't have to tell me. I'm just like you. I love traveling. Freddy always says, just give me a couple of trunks and a letter of credit, and I'm all right. Well, you ask Freddy. It's the funniest thing, but I was saying to him only last night at dinner—we were all alone, the Allens were coming, but their baby was sick at the last minute, the poor little thing, it's so delicate it would scare you to death to see it, oh, my God, I must call up Kate Allen and find out how it is, I told Freddy to remind me—I was telling him, 'One of these fine days,' I said, 'you won't see me sitting here,' I said. 'I'm going to just pack up a toothbrush and an extra pair of stockings,' I said, 'and the next you'll hear of me, I'll be in Egypt or India or somewhere,' I said. Oh, I'm a born traveler!"

"Really?" he said.

"Arabia!" she said. "Well, just imagine that. Tell me all about it. How did you like it, anyway?"

"Why, I had a good time," he said.

"Imagine," she said. "Way off there. Well, I've often wondered about Arabia. Tell me some more about it. Isn't there an awful lot of sand and everything?"

"Well, there is," he said. "But, you see—"

"Sand!" she said. "Don't sand me! After this summer down at Dune Harbor, I've had enough of sand, thank you. I could write a book about sand. Always in your shoes, no matter what you did, and the children tracking it into the house till I thought I'd go crazy. I did. I thought I'd simply go crazy. Ever been to Dune Harbor?"

"No," he said. "No, I haven't."

"Well, don't," she said. "Nothing but sand, sand, sand. You can get all the sand you want right there, without going off to any Arabia."

"Well, you see," he said, "the way it is in Arabia—"

"And Freddy on that beach!" she said. "You'd have died. The first day he got down there he just lay out there, and lay out there, and the first thing you knew, his shoulders! I thought about you, right away. I said if you could have seen those shoulders of his, you just simply would have died."

"It must have been awfully funny," he said. "You see, what I was going to say, in Arabia—"

"That's right," she said. "That's just exactly what I want you to do. Tell me all about your trip. I want to hear every single thing. What was it like? What are the people like? Are they all Arabs and everything?"

"Well, of course," he said, "there's a lot of—"

"Imagine!" she said. "Arabs! Isn't it exactly like something in a book? Oh, it must be just the way I pictured it. Tell me about all these Arabs. What are they like, anyway?"

"Why, they're pretty much like everybody else," he said. "Some of them are great, and some of them aren't so good. Most of them are pretty—"

"You know," she said, "I've always been sure I could get along with people like that. Arabs and everything. I'm so interested in people, they just seem to know, and they let me see their inside selves. Oh, I'm always making friends with the darndest people! You just ask Freddy. 'Well,' he said to me, 'nobody could ever call you a snob,' he said. And you know, I took it for a compliment. Arabs!

Oh, I'd love anything like that. Well, go on, tell me about it. Where did you stay?"

"Why, a lot of the time," he said, "I lived right with the natives. You see, I wanted to—"

"Imagine! Right with them!" she said. "But wasn't it terribly uncomfortable and everything?"

"They were darn decent to me," he said. "And as soon as you got used to it, you—"

"Oh, I could do it," she said. "I could do it in a minute. I don't care what I have to put up with, just as long as I'm traveling and seeing new things. When we were in Milan, three years ago, we went to this little hotel—the place was so crowded, there was nothing but Americans, wherever you went. I used to say to Freddy, 'You'd think some of them would have sense enough to stay home.' So we stayed at this little hotel, and do you know what we got? Well, I'll tell you, because you're an old friend, but if you ever—! We got fleas. Absolutely. Fleas. Freddy was nearly crazy, you know how he is, but I just said to him, 'Well, that's the kind of thing you've got to expect when you're traveling.' Oh, that's the way I am. Nothing fazes me. But look, these Arabs. Don't they all have a lot of wives or something?"

"Why, lots of them have more than one wife," he said. "You see, the way they look at it, it's a question of—"

"Aren't they terrible?" she said. "Imagine, more than one wife! Isn't that the Oriental of it, for you? They're terrible. And don't they all pretend to be terribly religious or something?"

"Their religion seems to mean a lot to them," he said. "No matter how poor a man is, or no matter where he goes, he always has his little mat, to—"

"Yes, I know," she said. "Prayer rugs. That's what they call them. Prayer rugs. I'll never forget, before I was married, we had this perfectly beautiful prayer rug in the living-room, right in front of the piano. We girls used to have a regular joke about it. We used to keep teasing Father, which one of us he was going to give it to—oh, he thought the world and all of that prayer rug! So then Father got married again, and of course, he kept the prayer rug right there. Oh, we often have a good laugh about that prayer rug!"

"Is that so?" he said.

"Oh, yes," she said. "My, that prayer rug! Oh, it was a beautiful thing, to anybody that appreciated it. Blue and yellow and I don't know what all colors. And everything in the design meant something.

Oh, they're awfully clever that way, those Arabs. They make some really lovely things. I suppose you've seen a lot of them."

"Yes," he said. "Yes, I have."

"I'm crazy about their work," she said. "I'd love to see them doing it. I've often thought, what I'd like to do, I'd like to—Oh, there's Freddy, over in the door. He wants to go home. Isn't he just the old stick-in-the-mud? Always wants to go home at half-past eleven. I say to him, 'You're as good as a clock,' I tell him. 'Whenever we're out at a party I can always tell when it's half-past eleven.' Honestly. I just tease the life out of him. But he never minds what I say. He just laughs. Well, I'm pretty dead, myself. Been shopping all day—it just kills me. I just put it off till the last minute, I hate it so. Now, listen, you've got to come and see us. We're pretty hurt, the way you've acted. Will you come soon? Please? Please?"

"Thank you very much," he said.

"And it was simply too wonderful," she said, "to hear all about Arabia. My, you've made me feel as if I was in an awful rut, just living here. But I'm going to do it some day. I warn you. One of these fine days you'll wake up and I'll be way off the other side of the world. That's the way I am—I've just got to do it, sooner or later. Will you look at Freddy scowling! He probably thinks you and I are fixing up a plan to elope, sitting here so long. Oh, he knows what you travelers are! Now you *are* coming soon, aren't you? There's heaps more things I want to ask you about. You needn't think you're done with Arabia yet, by any manner of means. You come soon! Now you mind Muvver! Don't you be bad, naughty, wicked, tebble boy ever adain. You hear me?"

"Thank you very much," he said.

"Nighty-ni'," she said. "S'eet d'eams."

"Good-night," he said.

She went on away to Freddy.

LUCKY LITTLE CURTIS

Mrs. Matson paused in the vestibule of G. Fosdick's Sons' Department Store. She transferred a small parcel from her right hand to the crook of her left arm, gripped her shopping-bag firmly by its German-silver frame, opened it with a capable click, and drew from its orderly interior a little black-bound book and a neatly sharpened pencil.

Shoppers passing in and out jostled her as she stood there, but they neither shared in Mrs. Matson's attention nor hurried her movements. She made no answer to the "Oh, I *beg* your pardons" that bubbled from the lips of the more tender-hearted among them. Calm, sure, gloriously aloof, Mrs. Matson stood, opened her book, poised her pencil, and wrote in delicate, prettily slanting characters: "4 crepe-paper candy-baskets, $.28."

The dollar-sign was gratifyingly decorative, the decimal point clear and deep, the 2 daintily curled, the 8 admirably balanced. Mrs. Matson looked approvingly at her handiwork. Still unhurried, she closed the book, replaced it and the pencil in the bag, tested the snap to see that it was indisputably shut, and took the parcel once more in her right hand. Then, with a comfortable air of duty well done, she passed impressively, and with a strong push, from G. Fosdick's Sons' Department Store by means of a portal which bore a placard with the request, "Please Use Other Door."

Slowly Mrs. Matson made her way down Maple Street. The morning sunshine that flooded the town's main thoroughfare caused her neither to squint nor to lower her face. She held her head high, looking about her as one who says, "Our good people, we are pleased with you."

She stopped occasionally by a shop-window, to inspect thoroughly the premature autumn costumes there displayed. But her heart was unfluttered by the envy which attacked the lesser women around her. Though her long black coat, of that vintage when coats were puffed of sleeve and cut sharply in at the waist, was stained and shiny, and her hat had the general air of indecision and lack of spirit that comes with age, and her elderly black gloves were worn in patches of rough gray, Mrs. Matson had no yearnings for the fresh, trim costumes set temptingly before her. Snug in her was the thought of the rows of recent garments, each one in its flowered cretonne casing, occupying the varnished hangers along the poles of her bedroom closet.

She had her unalterable ideas about such people as gave or threw away garments that might still be worn, for warmth and modesty, if not for style. She found it distinctly lower-class to wear one's new clothes "for every day"; there was an unpleasant suggestion of extravagance and riotous living in the practice. The working classes, who, as Mrs. Matson often explained to her friends, went and bought themselves electric ice-boxes and radios the minute they got a little money, did such things.

No morbid thought of her possible sudden demise before the clothes in her closet could be worn or enjoyed irked her. Life's uncertainty was not for those of her position. Mrs. Matsons pass away between seventy and eighty; sometimes later, never before.

A blind colored woman, a tray of pencils hung about her neck, with a cane tapping the pavement before her, came down the street. Mrs. Matson swerved sharply to the curb to avoid her, wasting a withering glance upon her. It was Mrs. Matson's immediate opinion that the woman could see as well as *she* could. She never bought of the poor on the streets, and was angry if she saw others do so. She frequently remarked that these beggars all had big bank-accounts.

She crossed to the car-tracks to await the trolley that would bear her home, her calm upset by her sight of the woman. "Probably owns an apartment-house," she told herself, and shot an angry glance after the blind woman.

However, her poise was restored by the act of tendering her fare to the courteous conductor. Mrs. Matson rather enjoyed small and legitimate disbursements to those who were appropriately grateful. She gave him her nickel with the manner of one presenting a park to a city, and swept into the car to a desirable seat.

Settled, with the parcel securely wedged between her hip and the window, against loss or robbery, Mrs. Matson again produced the book and pencil. "Car-fare, $.05," she wrote. Again the exquisite handwriting, the neat figures, gave her a flow of satisfaction.

Mrs. Matson, regally without acknowledgment, accepted the conductor's aid in alighting from the car at her corner. She trod the sun-splashed pavement, bowing now and again to neighbors knitting on their porches or bending solicitously over their iris-beds. Slow, stately bows she gave, unaccompanied by smile or word of greeting. After all, she was Mrs. Albert Matson; she had been Miss Laura Whitmore, of the Drop Forge and Tool Works Whitmores. One does not lose sight of such things.

She always enjoyed the first view of her house as she walked toward it. It amplified in her her sense of security and permanence. There it stood, in its tidy, treeless lawns, square and solid and serviceable. You thought of steel-engravings and rows of Scott's novels behind glass, and Sunday dinner in the middle of the day, when you looked at it. You knew immediately that within it no one ever banged a door, no one clattered up- and down-stairs, no one spilled crumbs or dropped ashes or left the light burning in the bathroom.

Expectancy pervaded Mrs. Matson as she approached her home. She spoke of it always as her home. "You must come to see me in my home some time," she graciously commanded new acquaintances. There was a large, institutional sound to it that you didn't get in the word "house."

She liked to think of its cool, high-ceilinged rooms, of its busy maids, of little Curtis waiting to deliver her his respectful kiss. She had adopted him almost a year ago, when he was four. She had, she told her friends, never once regretted it.

In her absence her friends had been wont to comment sadly upon what a shame it was that the Albert Matsons had no child—and with all the Matson and Whitmore money, too. Neither of them, the friends pointed out, could live forever; it would all have to go to the Henry Matsons' children. And they were but quoting Mrs. Albert Matson's own words when they observed that those children would be just the kind that would run right through it.

Mr. and Mrs. Matson held a joint view of the devastation that would result if their nephews and nieces were ever turned loose among the Matson and Whitmore money. As is frequent in such instances, their worry led them to pay the other Matson family the compliment of the credit for schemes and desires that had never edged into their thoughts.

The Albert Matsons saw their relatives as waiting, with a sort of stalking patience, for the prayed-for moment of their death. For years they conjured up ever more lurid pictures of the Matson children going through their money like Sherman to the sea; for years they carried about with them the notion that their demise was being eagerly awaited, was being made, indeed, the starting-point of bacchanalian plans.

The Albert Matsons were as one in everything, as in this. Their thoughts, their manners, their opinions, their very locutions were phenomena of similarity. People even pointed out that Mr. and Mrs. Matson looked alike. It was regarded as the world's misfortune that so obviously Heaven-made a match was without offspring. And of course—you always had to come back to it, it bulked so before you—there was all that Matson and Whitmore money.

No one, though, ever directly condoled with Mrs. Matson upon her childlessness. In her presence one didn't speak of things like having children. She accepted the fact of babies when they were shown to her; she fastidiously disregarded their mode of arrival.

She had told none of her friends of her decision to adopt a little boy. No one knew about it until the papers were signed and he was established in the Matson house. Mrs. Matson had got him, she explained, "at the best place in New York." No one was surprised at that. Mrs. Matson always went to the best places when she shopped in New York. You thought of her selecting a child as she selected all her other belongings: a good one, one that would last.

She stopped abruptly now, as she came to her gate, a sudden frown creasing her brow. Two little boys, too absorbed to hear her steps, were playing in the hot sun by the hedge—two little boys much alike in age, size, and attire, compact, pink-and-white, good little boys, their cheeks flushed with interest, the backs of their necks warm and damp. They played an interminable, mysterious game with pebbles and twigs and a small tin trolley-car.

Mrs. Matson entered the yard.

"Curtis!" she said.

Both little boys looked up, startled. One of them rose and hung his head before her frown.

"And who," said Mrs. Matson deeply, "who told Georgie he could come here?"

No answer. Georgie, still squatting on his heels, looked inquiringly from her to Curtis. He was interested and unalarmed.

"Was it you, Curtis?" asked Mrs. Matson.

Curtis nodded. You could scarcely tell that he did, his head hung so low.

"Yes, mother dear!" said Mrs. Matson.

"Yes, mother dear," whispered Curtis.

"And how many times," Mrs. Matson inquired, "have I told you that you were not to play with Georgie? How many times, Curtis?"

Curtis murmured vaguely. He wished that Georgie would please go.

"You don't know?" said Mrs. Matson incredulously. "You don't know? After all mother does for you, you don't know how many times she has told you not to play with Georgie? Don't you remember what mother told you she'd have to do if you ever played with Georgie again?"

A pause. Then the nod.

"Yes, mother dear!" said Mrs. Matson.

"Yes, mother dear," said Curtis.

"Well!" Mrs. Matson said. She turned to the enthralled Georgie. "You'll have to go home now, Georgie—go right straight home. And you're not to come here any more, do you understand me? Curtis is not allowed to play with you—not ever."

Georgie rose.

"'By," he said philosophically, and walked away, his farewell unanswered.

Mrs. Matson gazed upon Curtis. Grief disarranged her features.

"Playing!" she said, her voice broken with emotion. "Playing with a furnaceman's child! After all mother does for you!"

She took him by a limp arm and led him, unresisting, along the walk to the house; led him past the maid that opened the door, up the stairs to his little blue bedroom. She put him in it and closed the door.

Then she went to her own room, placed her package carefully on the table, removed her gloves, and laid them, with her bag, in an orderly drawer. She entered her closet, hung up her coat, then stooped for one of the felt slippers that were set scrupulously, in the first dancing position, on the floor beneath her nightgown. It was a lavender slipper, with scallops and a staid rosette; it had a light, flexible leather sole, across which was stamped its name, "Kumfy-Toes."

Mrs. Matson grasped it firmly by the heel and flicked it back and forth. Carrying it, she went to the little boy's room. She began to speak as she turned the door-knob.

"And before mother had time to take her hat off, too," she said. The door closed behind her.

She came out again presently. A scale of shrieks followed her.

"That will do!" she announced, looking back from the door. The shrieks faded obediently to sobs. "That's quite enough of that, thank you. Mother's had just about plenty for one morning. And today, too, with the ladies coming this afternoon, and all mother has to attend to! Oh, I'd be ashamed, Curtis, if I were you—that's what I'd be."

She closed the door, and retired, to remove her hat.

The ladies came in mid-afternoon. There were three of them. Mrs. Kerley, gray and brittle and painstaking, always thoughtful about sending birthday-cards and carrying glass jars of soup to the sick. Mrs. Swan, her visiting sister-in-law, younger, and given to daisied hats and crocheted lace collars, with her transient's air of bright, determined interest in her hostess's acquaintances and activities. And Mrs. Cook. Only she did not count very much. She was extremely deaf, and so pretty well out of things.

She had visited innumerable specialists, spent uncounted money, endured agonizing treatments, in her endeavors to be able to hear what went on about her and to have a part in it. They had finally fitted her out with a long, coiling, corrugated speaking-tube, rather like a larger intestine. One end of this she placed in her better ear, and the other she extended to those who would hold speech with her. But the shining black mouthpiece seemed to embarrass people and intimidate them; they could think of nothing better to call into it than "Getting colder out," or "You keeping pretty well?" To hear such remarks as these she had gone through years of suffering.

Mrs. Matson, in her last spring's blue taffeta, assigned her guests to seats about the living-room. It was an afternoon set apart for fancy-work and conversation. Later there would be tea, and two triangular sandwiches apiece made from the chopped remnants of last night's chicken, and a cake which was a high favorite with Mrs. Matson, for its formula required but one egg. She had gone, in person, to the kitchen to supervise its making. She was not entirely convinced that her cook was wasteful of materials, but she felt that the woman would bear watching.

The crepe-paper baskets, fairly well filled with disks of peppermint creams, were to enliven the corners of the tea-table. Mrs. Matson trusted her guests not to regard them as favors and take them home.

The conversation dealt, and favorably, with the weather. Mrs. Kerley and Mrs. Swan vied with each other in paying compliments to the day.

"So clear," said Mrs. Kerley.

"Not a cloud in the sky," augmented Mrs. Swan. "Not a one."

"The air was just lovely this morning," reported Mrs. Kerley. "I said to myself, 'Well, this is a beautiful day if there ever *was* one.'"

"There's something so balmy about it," said Mrs. Swan.

Mrs. Cook spoke suddenly and overloudly, in the untrustworthy voice of the deaf.

"Phew, this is a scorcher!" she said. "Something terrible out."

The conversation went immediately to literature. It developed that Mrs. Kerley had been reading a lovely book. Its name and that of its author escaped her at the moment, but her enjoyment of it was so keen that she had lingered over it till 'way past ten o'clock the night before. Particularly did she commend its descriptions of some of those Italian places; they were, she affirmed, just like a picture. The book had been drawn to her attention by the young woman at the Little Booke Nooke. It was, on her authority, one of the new ones.

Mrs. Matson frowned at her embroidery. Words flowed readily from her lips. She seemed to have spoken on the subject before.

"I haven't any use for all these new books," she said. "I wouldn't give them house-room. I don't see why a person wants to sit down and write any such stuff. I often think, I don't believe they know what they're writing about themselves half the time. I don't know who they think wants to read those kind of things. I'm sure *I* don't."

She paused to let her statements sink deep.

"Mr. Matson," she continued—she always spoke of her husband thus; it conveyed an aristocratic sense of aloofness, did away with any suggestion of carnal intimacy between them—"Mr. Matson isn't any hand for these new books, either. He always says, if he could find another book like *David Harum,* he'd read it in a minute. I wish," she added longingly, "I had a dollar for every time I've heard him say that."

Mrs. Kerley smiled. Mrs. Swan threw a rippling little laugh into the pause.

"Well, it's true, you know, it really is true," Mrs. Kerley told Mrs. Swan.

"Oh, it is," Mrs. Swan hastened to reassure her.

"I don't know what we're coming to, *I'm* sure," announced Mrs. Matson.

She sewed, her thread twanging through the tight-stretched circle of linen in her embroidery-hoop.

The stoppage of conversation weighed upon Mrs. Swan. She lifted her head and looked out the window.

"My, what a lovely lawn you have!" she said. "I couldn't help noticing it, first thing. We've been living in New York, you know."

"I often say I don't see what people want to shut themselves up in a place like that for," Mrs. Matson said. "You know, you exist, in New York—we live, out here."

Mrs. Swan laughed a bit nervously. Mrs. Kerley nodded. "That's right," she said. "That's pretty good."

Mrs. Matson herself thought it worthy of repetition. She picked up Mrs. Cook's speaking-tube.

"I was just saying to Mrs. Swan," she cried, and called her epigram into the mouthpiece.

"Live where?" asked Mrs. Cook.

Mrs. Matson smiled at her patiently. "New York. You know, that's where I got my little adopted boy."

"Oh, yes," said Mrs. Swan. "Carrie told me. Now, wasn't that lovely of you!"

Mrs. Matson shrugged. "Yes," she said, "I went right to the best place for him. Miss Codman's nursery—it's absolutely reliable. You can get awfully nice children there. There's quite a long waiting-list, they tell me."

"Goodness, just think how it must seem to him to be up here," said Mrs. Swan, "with this big house, and that lovely, smooth lawn, and everything."

Mrs. Matson laughed slightly. "Oh—well," she said.

"I hope he appreciates it," remarked Mrs. Swan.

"I think he will," Mrs. Matson said capably. "Of course," she conceded, "he's pretty young right now."

"So lovely," murmured Mrs. Swan. "So sweet to get them young like this and have them grow up."

"Yes, I think that's the nicest way," agreed Mrs. Matson. "And, you know, I really enjoy training him. Naturally, now that we have him here with us, we want him to act like a little gentleman."

"Just think of it," cried Mrs. Swan, "a child like that having all this! And will you have him go to school later on?"

"Oh, yes," Mrs. Matson replied. "Yes, we want him to be educated. You take a child going to some nice little school near here, say, where he'll meet only the best children, and he'll make friends that it will be a pretty good thing for him to know some day."

Mrs. Swan waxed arch. "I suppose you've got it all settled what he's going to be when he grows up," she said.

"Why, certainly," said Mrs. Matson. "He's to go right straight into Mr. Matson's business. My husband," she informed Mrs. Swan, "is the Matson Adding Machines."

"Oh-h-h," said Mrs. Swan on a descending scale.

"I think Curtis will do very well in school," prophesied Mrs. Matson. "He's not at all stupid—picks up everything. Mr. Matson is anxious to have him brought up to be a good, sensible business man—he says that's what this country needs, you know. So I've been trying to teach him the value of money. I've bought him a little bank. I don't think you can begin too early. Because probably some day Curtis is going to have—well——"

Mrs. Matson drifted into light, anecdotal mood.

"Oh, it's funny the way children are," she remarked. "The other day Mrs. Newman brought her little Amy down to play with Curtis, and when I went up to look at them, there he was, trying to give her his brand-new flannel rabbit. So I just took him into my room, and I sat him down, and I said to him, 'Now, Curtis,' I said, 'you must realize that mother had to pay almost two dollars for that rabbit—nearly two hundred pennies,' I said. 'It's very nice to be generous, but you must learn that it isn't a good idea to give things away to people. Now you go in to Amy,' I said, 'and you tell her you're sorry, but she'll have to give that rabbit right back to you.'"

"And did he do it?" asked Mrs. Swan.

"Why, I told him to," Mrs. Matson said.

"Isn't it splendid?" Mrs. Swan asked of the company at large. "Really, when you think of it. A child like that, just suddenly having everything all at once. And probably coming of poor people, too. Are his parents—living?"

"Oh, no, no," Mrs. Matson said briskly. "I couldn't be bothered with anything like that. Of course, I found out all about them. They were really quite nice, clean people—the father was a college man. Curtis really comes of a very nice family, for an orphan."

"Do you think you'll ever tell him that you aren't—that he isn't—tell him about it?" inquired Mrs. Kerley.

"Dear me, yes, just as soon as he's a little older," Mrs. Matson answered. "I think it's so much nicer for him to know. He'll appreciate everything so much more."

"Does the little thing remember his father and mother at all?" Mrs. Swan asked.

"*I* really don't know if he does or not," said Mrs. Matson.

"Tea," announced the maid, appearing abruptly at the door.

"Tea is served, Mrs. Matson," said Mrs. Matson, her voice lifted.

"Tea is served, Mrs. Matson," echoed the maid.

"I don't know what I'm going to do with her," Mrs. Matson told her guests when the girl had disappeared. "Here last night she had company in the kitchen till nearly eleven o'clock at night. The trouble with me is I'm too good to servants. The only way to do is to treat them like cattle."

"They don't appreciate anything else," said Mrs. Kerley.

Mrs. Matson placed her embroidery in her sweet-grass workbasket, and rose.

"Well, shall we go have a cup of tea?" she said.

"Why, how lovely!" cried Mrs. Swan.

Mrs. Cook, who had been knitting doggedly, was informed, via the speaking-tube, of the readiness of tea. She dropped her work instantly, and led the way to the dining-room.

The talk, at the tea-table, was of stitches and patterns. Praise, benignly accepted by Mrs. Matson, was spread by Mrs. Swan and Mrs. Kerley upon the sandwiches, the cake, the baskets, the table-linen, the china, and the design of the silver.

A watch was glanced at, and there arose cries of surprise at the afternoon's flight. There was an assembling of workbags, a fluttering exodus to the hall to put on hats. Mrs. Matson watched her guests.

"Well, it's been just too lovely," Mrs. Swan declared, clasping her hand. "I can't *tell* you how much I've enjoyed it, hearing about the dear little boy, and all. I *hope* you're going to let me see him some time."

"Why, you can see him now, if you'd like," said Mrs. Matson. She went to the foot of the stairs and sang, "*Cur*-tis, *Cur*-tis."

Curtis appeared in the hall above, clean in the gray percale sailor-suit that had been selected in the thrifty expectation of his "growing into it." He looked down at them, caught sight of Mrs. Cook's speaking-tube, and watched it intently, his eyes wide open.

"Come down and see the ladies, Curtis," commanded Mrs. Matson.

Curtis came down, his warm hand squeaking along the banister. He placed his right foot upon a step, brought his left foot carefully down to it, then started his right one off again. Eventually he reached them.

"Can't you say how-do-you-do to the ladies?" asked Mrs. Matson.

He gave each guest, in turn, a small, flaccid hand.

Mrs. Swan squatted suddenly before him, so that her face was level with his.

"My, what a nice boy!" she cried. "I just love little boys like you, do you know it? Ooh, I could just eat you up! I could!"

She squeezed his arms. Curtis, in alarm, drew his head back from her face.

"And what's *your* name?" she asked him. "Let's see if you can tell me what your name is. I just *bet* you can't!"

He looked at her.

"Can't you tell the lady your name, Curtis?" demanded Mrs. Matson.

"Curtis," he told the lady.

"Why, what a *pretty* name!" she cried. She looked up at Mrs. Matson. "Was that his real name?" she asked.

"No," Mrs. Matson said, "they had him called something else. But I named him as soon as I got him. My mother was a Curtis."

Thus might one say, "My name was Guelph before I married."

Mrs. Cook spoke sharply. "Lucky!" she said. "Pretty lucky, that young one!"

"Well, I should say so," echoed Mrs. Swan. "Aren't you a pretty lucky little boy? Aren't you, aren't you, aren't you?" She rubbed her nose against his.

"Yes, Mrs. Swan." Mrs. Matson pronounced and frowned at Curtis.

He murmured something.

"Ooh—*you*!" said Mrs. Swan. She rose from her squatting posture. "I'd like to *steal* you, in your little sailor-suit, and all!"

"Mother bought that suit for you, didn't she?" asked Mrs. Matson of Curtis. "Mother bought him all his nice things."

"Oh, he calls you mother? Now, isn't that sweet!" cried Mrs. Swan.

"Yes, I think it's nice," said Mrs. Matson.

There was a brisk, sure step on the porch; a key turned in the lock. Mr. Matson was among them.

"Well," said Mrs. Matson upon seeing her mate. It was her invariable evening greeting to him.

"Ah," said Mr. Matson. It was his to her.

Mrs. Kerley cooed. Mrs. Swan blinked vivaciously. Mrs. Cook applied her speaking-tube to her ear in the anticipation of hearing something good.

"I don't think you've met Mrs. Swan, Albert," remarked Mrs. Matson. He bowed.

"Oh, I've heard so much about Mr. Matson," cried Mrs. Swan. Again he bowed.

"We've been making friends with your dear little boy," Mrs. Swan said. She pinched Curtis's cheek. "You sweetie, you!"

"Well, Curtis," said Mr. Matson, "haven't you got a good-evening for me?"

Curtis gave his hand to his present father with a weak smile of politeness. He looked modestly down.

"That's more like it," summarized Mr. Matson. His parental duties accomplished, he turned to fulfill his social obligations. Boldly he caught up Mrs. Cook's speaking-tube. Curtis watched.

"Getting cooler out," roared Mr. Matson. "I thought it would." Mrs. Cook nodded. "That's good!" she shouted.

Mr. Matson pressed forward to open the door for her. He was of generous proportions, and the hall was narrow. One of the buttons-of-leisure on his coat-sleeve caught in Mrs. Cook's speaking-tube. It fell, with a startling crash, to the floor, and writhed about.

Curtis's control went. Peal upon peal of high, helpless laughter came from him. He laughed on, against Mrs. Matson's cry of "Curtis!," against Mr. Matson's frown. He doubled over with his hands on his little brown knees, and laughed mad laughter.

"Curtis!" bellowed Mr. Matson. The laughter died. Curtis straightened himself, and one last little moan of enjoyment escaped him.

Mr. Matson pointed with a magnificent gesture. "Upstairs!" he boomed.

Curtis turned and climbed the stairs. He looked small beside the banister.

"Well, of all the—" said Mrs. Matson. "I never knew him to do a thing like that since he's been here. I never heard him do such a thing!"

"That young man," pronounced Mr. Matson, "needs a good talking to."

"He needs more than that," his spouse said.

Mr. Matson stooped with a faint creaking, retrieved the speaking-tube, and presented it to Mrs. Cook. "Not at all," he said in anticipation of the thanks which she left unspoken. He bowed.

"Pardon me," he ordered, and mounted the stairs.

Mrs. Matson moved to the door in the wake of her guests. She was bewildered and, it seemed, grieved.

"I never," she affirmed, "never knew that child to go on that way."

"Oh, children," Mrs. Kerley assured her, "they're funny sometimes—especially a little boy like that. You can't expect so much. My goodness, you'll fix all that! I always say I don't know any child that's getting any better bringing up than that young one—just as if he was your own."

Peace returned to the breast of Mrs. Matson. "Oh—goodness!" she said. There was almost a coyness in her smile as she closed the door on the departing.

THE SEXES

THE YOUNG MAN with the scenic cravat glanced nervously down the sofa at the girl in the fringed dress. She was examining her handkerchief; it might have been the first one of its kind she had seen, so deep was her interest in its material, form, and possibilities. The young man cleared his throat, without necessity or success, producing a small, syncopated noise.

"Want a cigarette?" he said.

"No, thank you," she said. "Thank you ever so much just the same."

"Sorry I've only got these kind," he said. "You got any of your own?"

"I really don't know," she said, "I probably have, thank you."

"Because if you haven't," he said, "it wouldn't take me a minute to go up to the corner and get you some."

"Oh, thank you, but I wouldn't have you go to all that trouble for anything," she said. "It's awfully sweet of you to think of it. Thank you ever so much."

"Will you for God's sakes stop thanking me?" he said.

"Really," she said, "I didn't know I was saying anything out of the way. I'm awfully sorry if I hurt your feelings. I know what it feels like to get your feelings hurt. I'm sure I didn't realize it was an insult to say 'thank you' to a person. I'm not exactly in the habit of having people swear at me because I say 'thank you' to them."

"I did not swear at you!" he said.

"Oh, you didn't?" she said. "I see."

"My God," he said, "all I said, I simply asked you if I couldn't go out and get you some cigarettes. Is there anything in that to get up in the air about?"

"Who's up in the air?" she said. "I'm sure I didn't know it was a criminal offense to say I wouldn't dream of giving you all that trouble. I'm afraid I must be awfully stupid, or something."

"Do you want me to go out and get you some cigarettes; or don't you?" he said.

"Goodness," she said, "if you want to go so much, please don't feel you have to stay here. I wouldn't have you feel you had to stay for anything."

"Ah, don't be that way, will you?" he said.

"Be what way?" she said. "I'm not being any way."

"What's the matter?" he said.

"Why, nothing," she said. "Why?"

"You've been funny all evening," he said. "Hardly said a word to me, ever since I came in."

"I'm terribly sorry you haven't been having a good time," she said. "For goodness' sakes, don't feel you have to stay here and be bored. I'm sure there are millions of places you could be having a lot more fun. The only thing, I'm a little bit sorry I didn't know before, that's all. When you said you were coming over tonight, I broke a lot of dates to go to the theater and everything. But it doesn't make a bit of difference. I'd much rather have you go and have a good time. It isn't very pleasant to sit here and feel you're boring a person to death."

"I'm not bored!" he said. "I don't want to go any place! Ah, honey, won't you tell me what's the matter? Ah, please."

"I haven't the faintest idea what you're talking about," she said. "There isn't a thing on earth the matter. I don't know what you mean."

"Yes, you do," he said. "There's something the trouble. Is it anything I've done, or anything?"

"Goodness," she said, "I'm sure it isn't any of my business, anything you do. I certainly wouldn't feel I had any right to criticize."

"Will you stop talking like that?" he said. "Will you, please?"

"Talking like what?" she said.

"You know," he said. "That's the way you were talking over the telephone today, too. You were so snotty when I called you up, I was afraid to talk to you."

"I beg your pardon," she said. "What did you say I was?"

"Well, I'm sorry," he said. "I didn't mean to say that. You get me so balled up."

"You see," she said, "I'm really not in the habit of hearing language like that. I've never had a thing like that said to me in my life."

"I told you I was sorry, didn't I?" he said. "Honest, honey, I didn't mean it. I don't know how I came to say a thing like that. Will you excuse me? Please?"

"Oh, certainly," she said. "Goodness, don't feel you have to apologize to me. It doesn't make any difference at all. It just seems a little bit funny to have somebody you were in the habit of thinking was a gentleman come to your home and use language like that to you, that's all. But it doesn't make the slightest bit of difference."

"I guess nothing I say makes any difference to you," he said. "You seem to be sore at me."

"I'm sore at you?" she said. "I can't understand what put that idea in your head. Why should I be sore at you?"

"That's what I'm asking you," he said. "Won't you tell me what I've done? Have I done something to hurt your feelings, honey? The way you were, over the phone, you had me worried all day. I couldn't do a lick of work."

"I certainly wouldn't like to feel," she said, "that I was interfering with your work. I know there are lots of girls that don't think anything of doing things like that, but I think it's terrible. It certainly isn't very nice to sit here and have someone tell you you interfere with his business."

"I didn't say that!" he said. "I didn't say it!"

"Oh, didn't you?" she said. "Well, that was the impression I got. It must be my stupidity."

"I guess maybe I better go," he said. "I can't get right. Everything I say seems to make you sorer and sorer. Would you rather I'd go?"

"Please do just exactly whatever you like," she said. "I'm sure the last thing I want to do is have you stay here when you'd rather be some place else. Why don't you go some place where you won't be bored? Why don't you go up to Florence Leaming's? I know she'd love to have you."

"I don't want to go up to Florence Leaming's!" he said. "What would I want to go up to Florence Leaming's for? She gives me a pain."

"Oh, really?" she said. "She didn't seem to be giving you so much of a pain at Elsie's party last night, I notice. I notice you couldn't even talk to anybody else, that's how much of a pain she gave you."

"Yeah, and you know why I was talking to her?" he said.

"Why, I suppose you think she's attractive," she said. "I suppose some people do. It's perfectly natural. Some people think she's quite pretty."

"I don't know whether she's pretty or not," he said. "I wouldn't know her if I saw her again. Why I was talking to her was you wouldn't even give me a tumble, last night. I came up and tried to talk to you, and you just said, 'Oh, how do you do'—just like that, 'Oh, how do you do'—and you turned right away and wouldn't look at me."

"I wouldn't look at you?" she said. "Oh, that's awfully funny. Oh, that's marvelous. You don't mind if I laugh, do you?"

"Go ahead and laugh your head off," he said. "But you wouldn't."

"Well, the minute you came in the room," she said, "you started making such a fuss over Florence Leaming, I thought you never wanted to see anybody else. You two seemed to be having such a wonderful time together, goodness knows I wouldn't have butted in for anything."

"My God," he said, "this what's-her-name girl came up and began talking to me before I even saw anybody else, and what could I do? I couldn't sock her in the nose, could I?"

"I certainly didn't see you try," she said.

"You saw me try to talk to you, didn't you?" he said. "And what did you do? 'Oh, how do you do.' Then this what's-her-name came up again, and there I was, stuck. Florence Leaming! I think she's terrible. Know what I think of her? I think she's a damn little fool. That's what I think of her."

"Well, of course," she said, "that's the impression she always gave me, but I don't know. I've heard people say she's pretty. Honestly I have."

"Why, she can't be pretty in the same room with you," he said.

"She has got an awfully funny nose," she said. "I really feel sorry for a girl with a nose like that."

"She's got a terrible nose," he said. "You've got a beautiful nose. Gee, you've got a pretty nose."

"Oh, I have not," she said. "You're crazy."

"And beautiful eyes," he said, "and beautiful hair and a beautiful mouth. And beautiful hands. Let me have one of the little hands. Ah, look atta little hand! Who's got the prettiest hands in the world? Who's the sweetest girl in the world?"

"I don't know," she said. "Who?"

"You don't know!" he said. "You do so, too, know."

"I do not," she said. "Who? Florence Leaming?"

"Oh, Florence Leaming, my eye!" he said. "Getting sore about Florence Leaming! And me not sleeping all last night and not doing a stroke of work all day because you wouldn't speak to me! A girl like you getting sore about a girl like Florence Leaming!"

"I think you're just perfectly crazy," she said. "I was not sore! What on earth ever made you think I was? You're simply crazy. Ow, my new pearl beads! Wait a second till I take them off. There!"

ARRANGEMENT IN BLACK AND WHITE

THE WOMAN WITH the pink velvet poppies twined round the assisted gold of her hair traversed the crowded room at an interesting gait combining a skip with a sidle, and clutched the lean arm of her host.

"Now I got you!" she said. "Now you can't get away!"

"Why, hello," said her host. "Well. How are you?"

"Oh, I'm finely," she said. "Just simply finely. Listen, I want you to do me the most terrible favor. Will you? Will you please? Pretty please?"

"What is it?" said her host.

"Listen," she said. "I want to meet Walter Williams. Honestly, I'm just simply crazy about that man. Oh, when he sings! When he sings those spirituals! Well, I said to Burton, 'It's a good thing for you Walter Williams is colored,' I said, 'or you'd have lots of reason to be jealous.' I'd really love to meet him. I'd like to tell him I've heard him sing. Will you be an angel and introduce me to him?"

"Why, certainly," said her host. "I thought you'd met him. The party's for him. Where is he, anyway?"

"He's over there by the bookcase," she said. "Let's wait till those people get through talking to him. Well, I think you're simply marvelous, giving this perfectly marvelous party for him, and having him meet all these white people, and all. Isn't he terribly grateful?"

"I hope not," said her host.

"I think it's really terribly nice," she said. "I do. I don't see why on earth it isn't perfectly all right to meet colored people. I haven't any feeling at all about it—not one single bit. Burton—oh, he's just the other way. Well, you know, he comes from Virginia, and you know how they are."

"Did he come tonight?" said her host.

"No, he couldn't," she said. "I'm a regular grass widow tonight. I told him when I left, 'There's no telling what I'll do,' I said. He was just so tired out, he couldn't move. Isn't it a shame?"

"Ah," said her host.

"Wait till I tell him I met Walter Williams!" she said. "He'll just about die. Oh, we have more arguments about colored people. I talk to him like I don't know what, I get so excited. 'Oh, don't be so silly,' I say. But I must say for Burton, he's heaps broader-minded than lots of these Southerners. He's really awfully fond of colored people. Well, he says himself, he wouldn't have white servants. And you know, he had this old colored nurse, this regular old nigger mammy, and he just simply loves her. Why, every time he goes home, he goes out in the kitchen to see her. He does, really, to this day. All he says is, he says he hasn't got a word to say against colored people as long as they keep their place. He's always doing things for them—giving them clothes and I don't know what all. The only thing he says, he says he wouldn't sit down at the table with one for a million dollars. 'Oh,' I say to him, 'you make me sick, talking like that.' I'm just terrible to him. Aren't I terrible?"

"Oh, no, no, no," said her host. "No, no."

"I am," she said. "I know I am. Poor Burton! Now, me, I don't feel that way at all. I haven't the slightest feeling about colored people. Why, I'm just crazy about some of them. They're just like children—just as easy-going, and always singing and laughing and everything. Aren't they the happiest things you ever saw in your life? Honestly, it makes me laugh just to hear them. Oh, I like them. I really do. Well, now, listen, I have this colored laundress, I've had her for years, and I'm devoted to her. She's a real character. And I want to tell you, I think of her as my friend. That's the way I think of her. As I say to Burton, 'Well, for Heaven's sakes, we're all human beings!' Aren't we?"

"Yes," said her host. "Yes, indeed."

"Now this Walter Williams," she said. "I think a man like that's a real artist. I do. I think he deserves an awful lot of credit. Goodness, I'm so crazy about music or anything, I don't care *what* color he is. I honestly think if a person's an artist, nobody ought to have any feeling at all about meeting them. That's absolutely what I say to Burton. Don't you think I'm right?"

"Yes," said her host. "Oh, yes."

"That's the way I feel," she said. "I just can't understand people being narrow-minded. Why, I absolutely think it's a privilege to

meet a man like Walter Williams. Yes, I do. I haven't any feeling at
all. Well, my goodness, the good Lord made him, just the same as
He did any of us. Didn't He?"

"Surely," said her host. "Yes, indeed."

"That's what I say," she said. "Oh, I get so furious when people
are narrow-minded about colored people. It's just all I can do not
to say something. Of course, I do admit when you get a bad colored
man, they're simply terrible. But as I say to Burton, there are some
bad white people, too, in this world. Aren't there?"

"I guess there are," said her host.

"Why, I'd really be glad to have a man like Walter Williams come
to my house and sing for us, some time," she said. "Of course, I
couldn't ask him on account of Burton, but I wouldn't have any
feeling about it at all. Oh, can't he sing! Isn't it marvelous, the way
they all have music in them? It just seems to be right *in* them. Come
on, let's us go on over and talk to him. Listen, what shall I do when
I'm introduced? Ought I to shake hands? Or what?"

"Why, do whatever you want," said her host.

"I guess maybe I'd better," she said. "I wouldn't for the world
have him think I had any feeling. I think I'd better shake hands, just
the way I would with anybody else. That's just exactly what I'll do."

They reached the tall young Negro, standing by the bookcase.
The host performed introductions; the Negro bowed.

"How do you do?" he said.

The woman with the pink velvet poppies extended her hand at
the length of her arm and held it so for all the world to see, until the
Negro took it, shook it, and gave it back to her.

"Oh, how do you do, Mr. Williams," she said. "Well, how do
you do. I've just been saying, I've enjoyed your singing so awfully
much. I've been to your concerts, and we have you on the phonograph
and everything. Oh, I just enjoy it!"

She spoke with great distinctness, moving her lips meticulously,
as if in parlance with the deaf.

"I'm so glad," he said.

"I'm just simply crazy about that 'Water Boy' thing you sing,"
she said. "Honestly, I can't get it out of my head. I have my husband
nearly crazy, the way I go around humming it all the time. Oh, he
looks just as black as the ace of— Well. Tell me, where on earth do
you ever get all those songs of yours? How do you ever get hold of
them?"

"Why," he said, "there are so many different——"

"I should think you'd love singing them," she said. "It must be more fun. All those darling old spirituals—oh, I just love them! Well, what are you doing, now? Are you still keeping up your singing? Why don't you have another concert, some time?"

"I'm having one the sixteenth of this month," he said.

"Well, I'll be there," she said. "I'll be there, if I possibly can. You can count on me. Goodness, here comes a whole raft of people to talk to you. You're just a regular guest of honor! Oh, who's that girl in white? I've seen her some place."

"That's Katherine Burke," said her host.

"Good Heavens," she said, "is that Katherine Burke? Why, she looks entirely different off the stage. I thought she was much better-looking. I had no idea she was so terribly dark. Why, she looks almost like— Oh, I think she's a wonderful actress! Don't you think she's a wonderful actress, Mr. Williams? Oh, I think she's marvelous. Don't you?"

"Yes, I do," he said.

"Oh, I do, too," she said. "Just wonderful. Well, goodness, we must give someone else a chance to talk to the guest of honor. Now, don't forget, Mr. Williams, I'm going to be at that concert if I possibly can. I'll be there applauding like everything. And if I can't come, I'm going to tell everybody I know to go, anyway. Don't you forget!"

"I won't," he said. "Thank you so much."

The host took her arm and piloted her into the next room.

"Oh, my dear," she said. "I nearly died! Honestly, I give you my word, I nearly passed away. Did you hear that terrible break I made? I was just going to say Katherine Burke looked almost like a nigger. I just caught myself in time. Oh, do you think he noticed?"

"I don't believe so," said her host.

"Well, thank goodness," she said, "because I wouldn't have embarrassed him for anything. Why, he's awfully nice. Just as nice as he can be. Nice manners, and everything. You know, so many colored people, you give them an inch, and they walk all over you. But he doesn't try any of that. Well, he's got more sense, I suppose. He's really nice. Don't you think so?"

"Yes," said her host.

"I liked him," she said. "I haven't any feeling at all because he's a colored man. I felt just as natural as I would with anybody. Talked to him just as naturally, and everything. But honestly, I could hardly keep a straight face. I kept thinking of Burton. Oh, wait till I tell Burton I called him 'Mister'!"